Touchable/ Untouchable:

Dalit Literature from India in Translation

K. Satyanarayana
S. Shankar
GUEST EDITORS

S. Shankar
SERIES EDITOR

CONTENTS

Editor's Note

For this issue, I wear two hats—editor of the journal and editor of this issue, *Touchable/Untouchable: Dalit Literature from India in Translation.* I have worked with renowned Dalit Studies scholar and literary critic K. Satyanarayana to bring together five stunning Dalit literary works. It has long been a dream of mine to facilitate a publication of this kind, and it has been instructive as well as immensely pleasurable to work on it with Satya. Dalit literature deserves a wide readership, and I hope this issue enables it to reach many readers previously unfamiliar with it. Since Satya and I have provided a detailed introduction to the issue, I will resist saying more about it here.

Included in this issue are two new sections. The first, Literary Navigations, presents brief reflections on the craft and practice of producing and presenting literature in a global context. The plan is to make this section a regular feature of the journal. The second section presents the winning entries from the 2025 *Mānoa Journal* Contest. The remarkable winning entries were selected by Mai Der Vang (poetry) and Megan Kamalei Kakimoto (fiction). It is a distinct pleasure as well as an honor to present them here.

Acknowledging the members of the *Mānoa* team is a special pleasure of writing the Editor's Note. Siobhan Ting is a graduate assistant at the journal for 2025–2026. Michaela Gillan and Timmy Trần are both interns at the journal this year. All three of them have already begun making valuable contributions to the journal. We look forward to working with them through this year.

Adrian Khactu and Timmy are recipients of the Abernethy scholarship, housed in the journal.

S. Shankar
Honolulu, Hawaiʻi

Guest Editors' Introduction: Touchable/Untouchable: Dalit Literature from India in Translation

This issue of *Mānoa* presents Dalit literature from India in translation to a global audience of readers in English.

Why should readers outside India care about Dalit literature? For one thing, contemporary Dalit literature is among the most interesting and vibrant of literary enterprises currently underway in India. Contemporary Dalit literature has at one and the same time borne gripping witness to the centuries-old atrocious institution of exclusion and oppression known as caste, at the bottom of which Dalits are located as the most excluded and the most oppressed, and broken invigorating new literary ground. For these reasons alone, the value of reading Dalit literature should be evident. Dalit literature deserves a global audience, which it has begun to receive in recent years. This issue adds to Dalit literature's global reach in significant ways.

What does it mean to say Dalit works constitute a literature of witnessing? Not surprisingly—and here one might draw comparisons to slave narratives in the African American tradition—many early works of the contemporary boom in Dalit literature are testimonies, autobiographies, and memoirs. These works can certainly be read as testifying to the oppressive conditions under which Dalits and other "lower castes" live. As Omprakash Valmiki, celebrated Dalit author of the Hindi-language *Joothan*, declared in the preface to his autobiography, "After a long period of procrastination, I started to write. Once again, I had to relive all those miseries, torments, neglects, admonitions. I suffered a deep mental anguish while writing this book. How terribly painful was this unraveling of my self, layer upon layer" (p. viii).[1] The reader of this issue will find in the excerpts from Tulsiram's Hindi autobiography *Murdaihya*, as well as in Pradnya Daya Pawar's poem, a kind of biography-in-verse of a famous Dalit folk singer, fine examples of this kind of witnessing.

[1]Omprakash Valmiki, *Joothan: A Dalit's Life*, trans. Arun Prabha Mukherjee (Kolkata: Samya, 2007). Originally published in Hindi as *Joothan* in 1997.

On the other hand, literary critics have wondered whether the view of Dalit works as a literature of witnessing diminishes their aesthetic value. These critics have called their colleagues to account for having a unidimensional approach to Dalit literature—for essentially shoehorning Dalit works into a "witnessing" function. Because of the dangers of such shoehorning, it is important to recognize the many ways in which the literature produced by Dalits in the last fifty years challenges established literary conventions. For example, many Dalit writers eschew a high literary style, deliberately adopting in its place a vernacular/spoken one. The veteran Tamil writer Bama, an influence on the poet Sukirtharani, included here, is a case in point. Translator Lakshmi Holmstrom notes of her: "Bama is doing something completely new in using the demotic and the colloquial regularly .... She uses a Dalit style of language which overturns the decorum and aesthetics of received upper-class, upper-caste Tamil" (pp. x–xi).[2] Linguistically as well as formally, Dalit writers challenge contemporary Indian literature, as suggested by Baburao Bagul's essay in this issue ruminating on the aesthetics of Dalit literature.

In the end, both when it bears witness and when it innovates, Dalit literature presents a human story of struggle as well as triumph in startlingly powerful ways. This struggle is vividly brought out in the excerpts included in this issue from Bojja Tharakam's Telugu novel narrating the lives of a family of Dalit bonded laborers across generations. Of course, the same human story of struggle is found in different ways in all the pieces included. These human stories are also deeply Indian, as Indian as the more celebrated Indian writing in English, largely "upper caste," well known to global readers. The picture of India in Dalit literature may very well be familiar to readers in some respects. In others, to readers not familiar with Dalit literature, it will certainly be startling, evocative, shocking, moving, and more.

The term "Dalit literature" was coined in the first Dalit Literary Conference held in Mumbai (then Bombay) in 1958. Marathi Dalit writers created history by publishing several collections of poetry, short stories, autobiographical narratives, and critical essays in the 1960s and 1970s. *Poisoned Bread*, a classic anthology of these writings in English translation, was published in 1992. Marathi Dalit literature was widely translated into several Indian languages and served as an inspiration to Dalit writers in other Indian languages. Contemporary Dalit literature emerged as a powerful literary movement in Kannada, Telugu, Tamil, and Malayalam from the 1970s to the 1990s (see *No Alphabet in Sight* and *Steel Nibs*, coedited by K. Satyanarayana). It became a pan-Indian phenomenon with the rise of Dalit literatures in Hindi, Bengali, and other Indian languages after the 1990s. Dalit literature in English translation acquired a national and global

[2]Introduction to *Karukku* by Bama (Chennai: Macmillan, 2000).

visibility with the publication of autobiographies, novels, poetry, and essays by mainstream publishers.

Dalit literature is not simply a literary trend but a literary movement for social change. It describes and analyzes Dalit life worlds and struggles based on firsthand lived experience. The distinctive term "Dalit" (literally "crushed down" or "broken") is both identity and perspective. The Dalit Panthers, a group of insurgent intellectuals, popularized "Dalit" as a term to claim a dignified identity for "untouchables," while rejecting demeaning caste/jati names. They used the term to broadly refer to "untouchable" caste groups, Adivasis (aka "tribals"), and other minorities. In the course of history, "Dalit" became synonymous with the "untouchable" (in India also known as "scheduled caste") groups. Dalit critics theorized "Dalit" as a collective identity based on self-respect and human dignity. Dalit is a revolutionary term born out of anti-caste struggles and has shaped a Dalit perspective. In this sense, Dalit literature invents a canon and a normative Dalit character and inaugurates a shift from the old understanding of caste as a feudal relic to a contemporary form of power. It contests the view that untouchability is a cultural practice based on religious notions of "purity" and "impurity" and suggests that untouchability is a practice of social exclusion of Dalits from the public sphere.

Dr. B. R. Ambedkar (1891–1956) is a crucial pioneer of Dalit literature. Ambedkar was trained in the West and experienced caste discrimination. He developed critical concepts, such as the view of caste as "graded inequality," to analyze how inequality and discrimination were institutionalized by the sacred tradition. Ambedkar criticized the varna order (the idea of a social order of four varnas based on classical texts) because it is founded on inherited social status. Baburao Bagul and other Dalit critics were inspired by Ambedkar's language of equality and human worth and declared, "we too are human." Contemporary Dalit literature documents and examines descriptions of Dalit life in all its complexity and interprets caste as an undemocratic system based on graded inequality, divine retribution, and violence. It shares Ambedkar's view that caste is sanctified by Hindu feudalism.

Ambedkar is a critical figure for Dalit writers, as he formulated a critique of Indian literary history. He marked anti-colonial nationalism as Gandhian nationalism, which set up a binary opposition of the colonizer and the colonized. He shared the strategic view of colonialism as a structural break in Indian history that offered certain normative values to the oppressed. Canonical Indian literary texts portrayed an abstract Indian and excluded a vast section of Indians in order to obscure internal divisions based on caste, class, gender, and religion. This exclusion of Dalit and "lower" caste life from Indian literature cannot be viewed separately from the historical process of the formation of the canon of Indian/Gandhian literature. The Gandhian ideological hold is clear in the early Indian novels, where we find pitiable and submissive "lower" caste characters. For the first time, Dalit writers depicted autonomous and assertive Dalit characters in the 1960s. The Ambedkarite hero, to use Bagul's phrase, is a product of Ambedkarite thinking and the normative principles of equality and colonial modernity.

"Touchable/Untouchable: Dalit Literature from India in Translation" emerges out of this complex literary history. It takes a different approach to the presentation of Dalit literature to English-reading audiences than other recent efforts. Since anthologies presenting one or two works by a large number of writers already exist, we have chosen to present substantial work in translation from five celebrated contemporary Dalit writers: twenty-five poems in Tamil by Sukirtharani, translated by Anushiya Ramaswamy; two excerpts capable of standing by themselves from *Panchatantram*, a novel in Telugu by Bojja Tharakam, translated by Shirisha Amme; a creative/critical address on Dalit literature by the legendary writer Baburao Bagul, translated from Marathi by Maya Pandit; a long Marathi poem by Pradnya Daya Pawar, also translated by Maya Pandit; and an excerpt from *Murdahiya*, an autobiography in Hindi by Tulsiram, translated by Joel Lee. These works appear here for the first time in English.

Our intention has been to allow readers to dwell for a prolonged period of time in the imaginative spaces conjured up by these writers and their translators. This intention has been ably aided by the introductions to writers/works written by the translators. Hopefully, when readers listen in a sustained way to these literary voices with the help of the translator's introductions, they will begin to get a sense of the nuances of Dalit literature—its powerful witnessing, the freshness and boldness of its literary reimagining, and the productive ways in which the witnessing and the reimagining can be in tension with each other.

Also included in this issue is Siddhesh Gautam's striking artwork. Five images (one on the cover and four on interior pages) provide incisive commentary that complements the translations. Ambedkar figures prominently in these images (two of them cite him). The artwork is suffused in blue, the color of the Ambedkarite movement. Siddhesh Gautam is a Delhi-based artist, designer, writer, poet, and Ambedkarite. His artwork is informed by the anti-caste movement, and his work has been published in many mainstream publications. We offer them to the readers of this issue as powerful accompaniments to the literary work we have gathered. The ethos of this art aligns seamlessly with that of the literary works.

K. Satyanarayana and S. Shankar
Hyderabad and Honolulu

SIDDHESH GAUTAM

Artist's Statement

Siddhesh Gautam's art can be found on the cover and on pages 36, 79, 95, and 122.

The images I create are born out of both joy and struggle. Every drawing carries the weight of memory, of histories erased, of voices silenced, and yet the act of drawing—from reading to thinking to analyzing to rethinking and reimagining—itself is a kind of release—a way to breathe, to make space for stories that deserve to be seen through mediums such as poetry, scribbles, collages, and compositions on paper, cloth, mind, and digital screens. There is suffering in revisiting wounds of caste, in holding the pain of our people, and in remembering our own past experiences, but there is also joy in transforming that pain into lines, colors, and forms that speak back to power. The anti-caste movement, despite its revolutionary spirit, has often been denied a strong visual language. Our leaders, thinkers, and martyrs left behind words, songs, and ideas that continue to guide us, but the imagery to hold and carry them forward has remained scattered and incomplete. Through my work, I try to respond to this void—to draw for the movement, to give shape to memories, and to create icons and visions that can travel across generations.

My practice is my way of ensuring that the visual imagination of the anti-caste struggle grows as richly as its politics, so no child of ours feels unseen, unremembered, or orphaned of history. These illustrations are both personal reflections and collective memories—an attempt to locate myself within the long and living continuum of the anti-caste movement. Each image becomes a meditation on identity, memory, and liberation, echoing Dr. Ambedkar's call to "educate, agitate, organize." Through mirrors, hands, and the Ashoka Chakra, I explore how freedom is not only a public struggle but also an inward journey—a process of unlearning, remembering, and rebuilding the self.

In many ways, these are self-portraits—not always of my face, but of my position, my questions, and my desire to belong to a history of resistance. By placing fragments of myself—my hands, my body, my gaze—within these frames, I try to understand what it means to carry forward a movement that made my existence possible. The recurring blue and brown tones, like soil and sky, ground this world of Ambedkarite imagination—both earthly and transcendent. Through each line and color, I try to bridge the personal and the political, the intimate and the historical, reminding myself that the movement is not something outside of me—it lives within me, in every act of creation, reflection, and care.

Twenty-Five Tamil Poems

TRANSLATED BY ANUSHIYA RAMASWAMY

Translator's Note

The Tamil Dalit poet Sukirtharani's first experience of caste happened in second grade when she proffered a piece of store-bought "two cents candy" to a female classmate who had shared a similar sugar treat with her the day before. It was but a reciprocity, and yet, in an act of visible disgust, the girl slapped the offering out of Sukirtharani's hand and walked away, leaving the gift orphaned on the ground. In Sukirtharani's retelling, there still linger remnants of that cutting pain of public humiliation. She speculates that since there were only about ten Dalit families in her tiny North Tamil Nadu village of Lalapet, nestled near the larger township of Ranipet, during that time in the 1970s, she must have been pointed out as a child from the caste-segregated part of the village that is known as "ceri" in Tamil country. Maybe that six-year-old had mentioned Sukirtharani in her caste-Hindu home as a new friend, and her folks had used that opportunity to give her a primer on appropriate caste behavior, teaching their child her own caste name and place in society as essentially different from that of the Dalit-born.

In her poem, "Paraya Woman," Sukirtharani describes her school years in her village as a time of concerted denial of her home culture. The young one who had gleefully chased off crows as her father skinned the dead cow quickly learns as an adolescent to avoid him on the street as he wields the parai drum in village celebrations. And she, who had consistently scored the highest marks in her class, when alone made to sit in the last row with the boys, weeps in abject shame after refusing to admit to her father's caste-based work. In a modern Indian culture that allows mobility for white-collar work, the hereditary professions that play a foundational part in village ceremonies are reserved only for the Dalit working castes. To these subaltern castes belong the barber called to shave the head of the new baby or of the oldest son of the dead patriarch, the local washerwoman participating in the purification rites of a puberty ceremony, and, most importantly, the drummer producing the unmistakable sound of parai drumming ubiquitous at the annual festival of the village deity and at every funeral house signifying the presence of death. While certain skills such as working with gold and iron are indeed pedagogically passed down in families as in European medieval guilds, the Dalit-associated tasks are a demand placed by a collective caste ethos. Sukirtharani's father had a day job at the local Parry's ceramic factory and yet was called upon periodically to perform the parai as his traditional caste duty. The duty is a moral imperative backed by thin-skinned violence.

At the heart of Sukirtharani's poetry lies her conviction that "caste is grown in the village," as if it is a local produce like eggplant or chilies. Nietzsche's The Genealogy of Morals *proposes a primal moment of debt, of a promise to pay that is burned into the self of the borrower through an act of memory, as the birth of guilt and conscience. And yet, in the context of caste, this archaic promise is kept alive conscientiously, not by the mythic borrower, that ancient first Dalit, but by the caste Hindu. The demand for caste-based work from the Dalit as a recompense for some unknown injury now lost in the mists of history, a feudalistic corvée labor that continues to this day as an ethical duty, runs counter to all modern notions of justice and human rights.*

For Sukirtharani, her ethos as a Dalit feminist poet is fundamental to her self-account. Dispossessed as a Dalit and a woman in a village culture that justifies its anachronistic gender/caste subjections according to a set of universal norms backed by scripture, Sukirtharani insists on claiming an identity that is one of discomfort and mourning. Her critics run the gamut from those who click their tongues over her speaking of the vicissitudes of the female body (using euphemisms like "raw") to the cultural conservatives who frown upon her polemical critiques of a patriarchal, elitist, caste-supremacist national imaginary. Sukirtharani, like the German-born Jewish philosopher Hannah Arendt before her, argues that since it is on the grounds of descent that she is oppressed, her poetry too should be grounded on the same identity that makes her an abject object. For in lived Indian culture, Hindu cultural practices are an unending series of caste performances signifying and dividing the material world into the touchable/untouchable. For even though "Dalit" is a collective noun signifying a multitudinous group of different castes that are designated as "untouchable" (as Dalit work often involves manual cleaning labor, this appellation is another piece of the caste justificatory edifice built out of commonsensical norms), Dalit castes are also internally separated and hierarchized from each other, leading to further isolation that inhibits civic collective bargaining. "There is no garbage collection in my ceri," Sukirtharani notes wryly.

There is a "calm violence" (Foucault's description for something else) to the everyday life of the Indian village, with the village proper of the caste Hindus functioning as the sovereign. If Sukirtharani wished, she could simply move to an urban milieu and practice a de-casted proto-Hinduism (from marriage practices to naming protocols, it would mean taking on a mainstream, unmarked identity that signals an unexpressed Dalitism: in other words, passing as a caste Hindu). Instead, she lives as a single woman and teaches at the same school where she suffered a thousand cuts, a space that still presses on her to stay in her place at the bottom. Even now, Sukirtharani admits, she would not be able to rent or buy a home outside the ceri, as that would destroy the mapped caste lines of Lalapet. The last line in her "Returning Home" poem is an eviscerating critique of this lived reality—her progressive compatriot, a caste Hindu, after an exhilarating political meeting exhorting a local community to move toward an equitable world promised by modern democracy, returns to his home in the village proper, while Sukirtharani, who had been standing and speaking as an equal next to him, leaves for her ceri.

Pushing the Dalit families into an encampment outside the village proper is a refusal of a common ancestor, for the Dalit presence denies the homology of the village. If there is one belief that unites the various castes living within the village proper, divvying up their share of power and claims to a regional identity, it is this refusal to accept the Dalit within a shared Hindu varna system, that ontogenesis of the male human body quartered and siloed into socially valuable professions. The desperately necessary work of any human inhabitation involving the removal of the dead, dirt, and night soil is then forced onto those defined as the Dalit. Sukirtharani's poem, "The House on My Back," speaks of this burden of carrying the weight of a "tightly locked house" on her back. Her metaphor reminds us of the intimacy of the domestic, the silences involved in cleaning, and the despair of the porter that remains unacknowledged. Her poems, even the ones that might be denoted as "love poems," challenge the practices of effacement that caste performances polish and renew even in times of political liberalization.

Sukirtharani came of age in the heyday of Tamil Dalit literature in the 1990s, profoundly impacted by the novels of Bama and Sivakami (Sukirtharani calls these pioneer Tamil Dalit female writers her "akkas," or older sisters) that fundamentally changed the Tamil literary landscape. She was in her mid-twenties when she wrote "Paratchi," translated here as "Paraya Woman," sharply recognizing the caste interpellation as one that functioned as an affirmation of non-Parayar ontology. Each time the word was enunciated, that question of "who speaks" becomes a rhetorical unsaid for the caste certainty of the non-Dalit, referring usually in the most mundane manner to a neighbor.

The poem functions as a triptych: it is at first reading a coming-of-age narrative registering a particular subjectivity through a series of easily recognizable caste experiences (the father's Nandan-like working with leather, the alms-rice, the parai, the back bench banishment, and the ontological question), while it is also an apologia for the actions of an unthinking younger self. But most resoundingly, it is a political manifesto of disruptive rhetoric. For Sukirtharani is clearly aligning herself with her akkas. In beginning the poem with her father's work cutting and curing animal skin, Sukirtharani points to the dominant culture's disinterest in the knowledges of the underclass, treating Dalit work in the material world as lacking any kind of epistemic validity. One remembers that the wisest figure in the Black novelist Ralph

Ellison's The Invisible Man *is the junk man, with his plaintive blues lyrics and a cart full of blueprints thrown out of corporate office buildings as trash. Sukirtharani's poems, like the novels of Bama and Sivakami, uncover alternative and suppressed knowledges as a literary poetics.*

Caste, like race, functions as singular and absolute for each individual. How does one learn to apprehend one's life as a caste minority? One is born into a caste, whose framework functions as a precondition to one's birth and death. The poem "Storm Sign," like "Possible Sex," describes the impossibility of love between a couple divided by the chasms of gender and caste. These poems are paeans to mourning, like Du Bois's in The Souls of Black Folk, *where his descriptions of racial discrimination—his own, most memorably—appear not so much to prove the claim that African Americans are treated with bias but to theorize on the psychobiography of a people who live in terror of a white majority.*

In Sukirtharani's head live the litany of names and details of Dalit women spectacularly disarticulated by their caste Hindu neighbors. Their hometowns range all over the modern Indian map. She mentions Priyanka, that seventeen-year-old Dalit girl from Khairlanji, whose body was fished out of the local canal with sticks and rods stuck between her legs. The local authorities, from the police to the doctors who performed the autopsy, swore that there was no rape, though Priyanka and her mother, Surekha, had been paraded through their village streets naked. Sukirtharani's poem "A Paratchi Can Commit Murder Too," with its propulsive inventory of extreme harm done to the Dalit body, describes the serial killer-style cruelties done to Dalit women in broad daylight as caste and gender punishment. It is salutary to remember that the year Sukirtharani was in second grade, the Supreme Court of India reversed the lower court punishment of the two policemen found guilty of raping the fourteen-year-old Mathura on the grounds that due to her caste origins, the teenager was promiscuous and had probably "incited the two drunk policemen to sex." The huge uproar over these words that reflect all the biases of a hierarchically organized social system, where some victims cannot be recognized as precarious and therefore as "injurable" (Judith Butler's inimitable words that fit Mathura perfectly), changed rape law in India in the 1980s and led to the rise of organized women's movements all over the nation.

Sukirtharani lives and writes now in a time where neoliberal economic policies have created a sense of infinite consumer choices and of modern modes of community building that insist on the possibility of other identities in cyberspaces. Sukirtharani sees these calls to move beyond, to enter a post-period, whether in terms of caste/race or war, as the prerogative of the dominant. Her vision of hope lies in the future, when a new language, "still sticky with blood," will be born, when an earth with the man-drawn maps of borders has been erased, and when the rise of a forest will transform us into reflecting its abundance and generosity. We wait with her.

PARAYA WOMAN

When the dead cow
gets skinned
I would stand there
chasing crows

I would eat
the begged rice
alms claimed
after a long wait
and boast it was hot

If I happen to see
my father
with his parai drum
on the street
I would cover
my face and pass

Unable to name
my father's profession
and admit
his yearly income
I get a beating
from the teacher

Forced to sit
in the last row
without any female friends
I would weep in silence.

But now
if someone
were to ask
I reply
brightly
that I am a Paratchi.[1]

---

[1]The Tamil word is the female version of the now Anglicized global term for social ostracization, "Pariah."

PARAYA GOD

When the sun burns
enough to stretch the back
You call that a paraya sun.

When the drying ripe grains
are pecked and swept away
That's a paraya crow.

When what's in hand
gets grabbed off the wrist
It's a paraya dog.

If the ground is plowed
and planted with sweat
What else but a paraya labor.

If everything is named thus
What is that paraya god
steeped in blood frenzy?

THE NAKEDNESS OF THE PAGES

After your ejections
have stained my deep
dark recesses
you fall asleep
and on the spread
of waves
that have been pressed
down and blunted
by your weight
I write the tales
of the vanquished
in a loud yellow

The ink of the
writings glitter

When your back sweats
and you turn over
you get struck by the power
of my lightning and awaken
nature takes its course
chapters get exchanged
and the corrections begin
from the fertilized egg
the backbone of the words
get broken
their meanings
get hidden
massive chasms
get filled with your
malicious waters
Finally
when somehow your acid
stops dripping
everything underlined
has been destroyed

The nakedness of those pages
watch you with contempt
as you snore in your sleep.

POSSIBLE SEX

When you enter my room
the lack of four walls
registers in your amazed eye
Is it possible to have a room
without walls?
You are confused
The light of your arrival
announces that
there are no doors
Stars fall from the roof
Underfoot the floor
slips like a dog's skin
When the molecules inside
your cells begin to stretch
The open field where dragonflies
roam makes you cringe
with shame
So you invite me
I who am decorated
with living trees
to your air-conditioned
liquid glass-screened place

My cheeks tremble
and shake
with my laughter
For you
who sharpens
your prick
on a roadside rock
for whom
sex is possible anywhere

A YOUNG LANGUAGE

I want a language
no one has ever spoken before
A language beyond the meanings
created by symbols and gestures
A language that floats in the uterus

That
would have the decency
not to search
through my torn underwear
to my privates

Will have a thousand words
that cannot be used
to stab me in my back
as I pass by

Will not give meaning
to all those late-night dreams
that are kept in mind
only to be shared
as just lamentations

Its meanings stretch sky-wide
Its soft words
will not wound
the tongue's thin skin

The keys
of that special language
will destroy tears
and give birth to valor

You will see the beginnings
of my alphabet in it
and be terrified
You will beg me
in your sour and bitter
tasting rotten language
to return to those
blackened pieces of glass

Of that too
I would write about openly
in my young language
still sticky with blood.

DEATH

When crossing through
the mature mesquite jungle
a moan comes floating
That was when I met it
in that interval
between sensing
my humid breaths
Lying half dead
there is a commanding plea
bursting from its eyes
I cradle it in my palm
and carry it to my room
Hesitant and surprised
it sits down
My compassion
as I tended its wounds
must have charmed it
Then we slept
close to each other
Rescuing extinct stories
we talked to each other
through the night
The teacup became common
to all four lips
One day it brought
a broken-off piece of lightning
to prove its power
When I began to weep
Death took me away
to its home in gratitude.

STORM SIGN

My unshaven nakedness
is as majestic
as undestroyed forests
You stand afar
and dig at my body
submerged
in the color
of nature's bud
with your sling stick

Like water
saved in rocky
crevices
that has never
drunk light
I welcome you
in a language
that has not lost its value
The sharpness of my eye
makes your genitals falter
My song carrying the sound
of a tall tree felled
with a sharp saw
makes you angry
you bury your head
in breasts that had never
known teeth marks
and raise it over
a dried skin
dead to lust
My fingers stretch
sharp as green cactus

Tightening your
undone clothing
You run along city streets
shouting that a tribal
woman is crossing
the border.

TREATY

A treaty
between the two of us.
That for some time
You live as me
and I live as you.
On an evening
at the end of the treaty
period
we meet,
You as you
And I as I.

WITH MY HANDS FILLED WITH POEMS

I am coming to you
with an infinite
number of kisses
You too come
toward me
In one kiss
many poems
and in one poem
many kisses
fall away
unable to hold on.

FIRST KISS

It has been many days
since we shared kisses

Like an umbilical cord
cut off with a sharpened rock
a kiss has been fluttering
between our lips

Each time
it happens
it is a dry kiss
of blocked
blood flow

The sound of that kiss
received from touched lips
hits the empty wall
and rebounds
in the grand howl
of a battleground

A kiss
not sipped from touch
lies there dry
as a light ray

When awake
the mirage lips
do a lockdown

At inopportune moments
while catching a nap
curved out like convex mirrors[2]
our first kiss
from long ago
fills the empty space

---

[2]The Tamil word for mirror is *kannaadi*—with a hard stress on the "n" sound. The poem removes the "kann" part (which means "eye") and instead uses the word for convex mirror: "valaintha aadi." Once an image pops into the mind of a body tilted backward, sleeping on a train maybe, the line makes perfect sense.

A HOUSE ON MY BACK

Something
as thick as mercury
presses into the skin
of my fleshy back.

I push my hand
behind
and feel around
There is a tightly
locked house there.

On top of it
an eternally weeping
one-legged bird of time

Inside the stone walls
of the room lies the key
to the locked house

All the narrow corridors
between the rooms
like the blood veins
of the heart
open into a dark room
with an exhaust fan

The library's
gorgeous books
travel in the septic tanks

Unable to bear
this life-squeezing torture
I fling word bombs behind

The house bursts into pieces
The back begins to straighten.

LOVE OF WRITING

To live with it
is the torture
of having
a foot caught
in a landmine.
Its intercessions
of introducing me
to everyone
have increased.
It sucks up my conscious
thoughts by soaking
me fully in my secret acts
and in the bitter intoxication
of black liquor spilling
down the glass.
It enters my private room
as unfiltered air
leaving its jealous
footprints on
wet bathroom floors.
Late at night
It takes over my shuddering body
and does its wild dance
I drown it
in the drain
in the empty field
and return home.
But there it sits
cross-legged in the living room
the love of writing I'd abandoned.

THE DEATH OF ANCIENT WORDS

I am a collector
of ancient words
On a long night
in the ruins
of a pavilion hall
the moldy words
began to be collected.

While traveling
through forests
archaic words bursting
with secrets were found
with their root matter

Then
in the cursed desert
after digging deep
I gathered
teeth-marked words
out of preserved mouths

In green fields
along with the grains
chewed and spat out
by the fairies
were some spilled words.
As the words
kept increasing
the backpack
began to swell

when crossing
a breathtaking chasm
unable to bear the
combined weight of the words
I left them to ford the river

When I came back
the words had been
hung to death.

THE FOREST'S FAREWELL

Like a dried seed
from a bursting pod
I fly and fall
within you
with no prior
warning

Without any shock
you unlock
the green screen
from inside

Once my pupils
stop dilating
and I become attuned
to the gentle darkness
you show me
each of the rooms
built without bricks

You are overflowing
with the unrecordable
primordial melody
of a wooden music box

The wings of all
the birds pierce
your back as they fly

You swiftly slice
into yourself
to exhibit age rings
older than soil

Slowly your greenness
begins to spread over me
I lean over and look
at my body
in the mirror
of stagnant water
held by a root

There is a tip
of a bud
on the head
and a branching root
at the foot.

THE RUN

My run has many
complicated rules.

A win involves
no one else losing
To lose means
there should be
no winner.

The mind may
decide the distance
and the feet may mark
the starting point.

The eye may choose
the path of the run:
a riverbank,
a forest way
untouched by light,
a track along ash stained
molten lava rock
or a private trail
through an antediluvian garden.

If unable to cross
one may rest halfway
The hands of Time
have no stopwatch.

Even the distance
of the return
will be added
to the outbound
journey.

There will be no
hand gestures
or waving flags
signaling the end
of the run

Then
what will
judge me?
When I am
not there
your footprints
gathered
at my starting point.

THE SOUND OF FIRE BURNING

I am not going
to be worried
about your actions

You have buried
my body
in the depths of the land
that gaped its mouth
open in shock

You have filled
a polished glass jar
with my words
to roll it between
your feet in play.

All my cool truths
you break
by blowing on them
with your smelly mouth
breath

Only your reflection
fills my eyes
You ask
what can you do
in the world
without me?
You are a terrible person.
Even to fuck
you have a thousand ways
When your organs go slack
and you are ensconced
on the hill of ennui
you will dig in the place
of burial.
I will then appear
transformed by
millennially formed abilities

With your uncovered ears
You cannot avoid hearing
The sound of fire burning.

THE VALOR OF VULVAS[3]

In an evolution
after many millennia
useless
your phallus will disappear
at that moment
your heirs will comprehend
the valor of our vulvas.

[3]These poems so far are from Sukirtharani's second poetry collection, "Iravu Mirugam" ("Night Animal"), published by Kalachuvadu Publications, Nagercoil, in 2004.

THE EARTH[4]

I remember
hearing somewhere
that the earth is round
But
however
I kneel,
bend down,
twist
and look
It looks square
through the window
of my house.

[4]From http://arputharaju.blogspot.com/2021/05/blog-post_19.html.

A PARATCHI CAN COMMIT MURDER TOO[5]

You strip our clothes
make us naked
Rape us
Order us
to fuck
our older brother
Push a steel hook
into our vaginas
Cut off our breasts
and throw them
into canals
Fling acid
Chop off our heads
Slice away the leg
Make the corpse
disappear
Stuff shit into mouths
Force feed piss
Call it a *ceri*
and segregate it
Place a garland
of footwear around
our necks
Call out "Whore"
"Paraiya"
Set us on fire
Hang us on trees
Build a wall of untouchability
Give us a separate drinking cup
Ban us from wearing footwear
When we fall in love
you call it a melodrama
Commit honor killing
Now there is nothing more
left for you to do.

---

[5]These poems are from the poetry collection "Ippadikku Eval" ("Yours, Eve"), published in May 2016 by Kalachuvadu Publications, Nagercoil, Tamil Nadu.

But for me?
A *Paratchi* can commit murder too.[6]

[6]This line is a play on a common Tamil saying: "A Pathini (chaste woman) is capable of murder too." In translating this statement, with its archaic resonance, I used the contextual meaning of the original "pathini" saying: that in an untenable situation, even the chaste woman is capable of the ultimate act of violence.

FRESH BLOOD

I am like a young cactus
born from the shriveled skin
of the vast desert
I don't need
the raindrop
that comes discolored
out of the sandstorm
or the water buried deep
between the rocks
I never look up at the
color of the heat
dripping over me all the time
Even the last drop of cool night air
that marks the end of the day's heat
leaves me untouched
When the wind flings
the sand with a heavy hand
my skin only glistens more
my shallow roots
sharpen their ends
my red fruits
thornless
are ripe for eating

When you
come from far
cut me and lay
me on the ground
out bursts and leaks
the sticky
fresh blood.

THE ABANDONED TOMB

Like a drop of water hanging
on the edge of a leaf
the soul is moaning
as it gazes at its body
laid out afar
As if a wound is sliced
into without morphine
right in front of its eyes
it lets its life drain away.

Let my body lie
at the base of the blue-painted
snow mountain
where each mountain
splits and separates
itself from each other.

When I was born
it was said
that I opened my eyes
when a drop of ice
was placed on my tongue.
The memory
of my childhood spent
playing with lambs
is frozen on the mountain's lap.
It wiped away
the first blood
that spurted at puberty

I have flung my writings
there like feed to doves

If anybody crosses here
point out that
there is an abandoned tomb
over there.

MY NAME IS RIVER

The moon cannot be seen
during the day
Like saying the Sun is red
I have always been here

When was I born
How did I grow up
When I reached puberty
Who hugged and kissed me
I do not know
Like the continuous melt
of a snowcapped mountain
I float like a leaf
bloom into waves
bud forth in froth
ripen all over my body
with sand
like your night vine
I spread everywhere
you embrace me
eat me
split me into two

You are swimming
in me
I enter
through the mountain
gap and come out
you stretch me
like you please
you put your hand
in my lap
pluck the ripened
sand fruits
with their stems on
and run away
while I am left standing
my body dried up
tongue parched
my veins bloodless
I am water's tomb.

A POEM OF YOU AND I

You are the unknown origin
Of a spring that never runs dry

I am the soft place where
a breathlessly rushing river
mingles with the sea

Between us swings
this poem
moving like a snake
seeking its pair.

RETURNING HOME

We roam
bilious in our belief
that speech and writing
are weapons
The world could be held
within our palms
that it would roll
in the direction blown
In the future,
like glowworms buried in clay
villages would gleam
People gather
when we call out
that it is possible
to even out
society's potholes

A tea shop springs up
people sit picking
out rocks from raw
rice for tomorrow's cooking
children fall asleep
men lie on the ground to listen
Those sitting on tree branches
cannot see the crows.

At dawn,
The worry of bringing home
the grown paddy and cleaned air
torment the folks

There is a hair salon
open even at this hour

Everyone claps as
stiff as a corpse
set to burn on the pyre

Both of us step down
from the stage
orderly rows disrupted
folks disperse
You go into the village
I leave for the *ceri.*

LET'S KILL THE FATHERS

That was the time
of dragonflies
From then on
I began going with mother
to the fallow fields
She was never worried
about her dried as a seed
body as she pulled up
by the roots
the stones of sorrow
grown knee-high
The sky was empty
of clouds above her
sun-heated head
By then I'd caught
a dragonfly

As she continued
to make tools of her hands
I had never seen before
on our lands
such a sublime rainfall
an overflowing harvest
When the sun began to
slowly deck itself
with night
she was speaking
of the pressing yoke
the dispossession
of ancient land
she was flowing
like a dammed river
I whisper softly
in her ears
Let's kill the fathers.

BOJJA THARAKAM

The Body on Fire & The Strength of Ten Elephants

EXCERPTS FROM THE TELUGU NOVEL *PANCHATANTRAM*
TRANSLATED BY AMME SHIRISHA

Translator's Note

Bojja Tharakam (1939–2016) was a poet, novelist, translator, and political activist. He belonged to Kandikuppa in the East Godavari district of the South Indian state of Andhra Pradesh. His father, Bojja Appalaswamy, was a schoolteacher and a political figure who started the Ambedkar-led Scheduled Caste Federation in their area in 1942. He was elected to the Madras State Legislative Assembly in 1952 and the Andhra Pradesh Assembly in 1955. Tharakam's mother, Mavullamma, did not attend school, but with the help of her husband, she learned to read and write. Tharakam studied in a school set up by his father for Dalit children in his village. Later, he continued his schooling at Pithapuram Raja's School in Kakinada. During his college days at PR Government College in Kakinada, he was a student activist for the Republican Student Federation and became its district president. Tharakam studied law at Osmania University, Hyderabad. In 1968, he married his classmate, Vijayabharathi, whose father was also a well-known Dalit poet, Boyi Bhimanna. Bhimanna was a government translator and offered Tharakam a day job as a junior translator. Tharakam entered a new phase in his life in the mid-1960s. He began his career as an advocate in the district court of Kakinada in 1965 and in 1968 moved to Nizamabad, where he continued his legal practice till 1978.

Tharakam conducted many sessions related to Ambedkar in universities, and students felt connected to these sessions. He was inspired by the Dalit Panther movement in Maharashtra, which was at its height in the late 1960s and early 1970s. The Ambedkar Yuvajana Sangham (Ambedkar Youth Forum), a district-level organization with branches in many villages, was formed. Through this organization, many campaigns were conducted against caste atrocities. Both as a lawyer and a political leader, Tharakam was active in the movement. As president of the AP Beedi Workers' Union in Nizamabad, Adilabad, and Karimnagar, Tharakam took part in the forty-day strike demanding the implementation of the Beedi and Cigar Workers Act of 1964. His involvement with the Raithu Coolie Sangham landed him in jail during the Emergency in July 1975. He was detained under the Maintenance of Internal Security Act and the Defence of India Act till July 1976. During this phase, Tharakam was vice-president of the Andhra Pradesh Civil Liberties Committee (APCLC) and a member of the Revolutionary Writers' Association. In 1978, he contested from Nizamabad as an independent candidate supported by the Communist Party of India (Marxist–Leninist).

Tharakam was a key figure in moving Dalit groups from presenting memoranda to the government, or trying to get things done through their contacts with ministers and officials, to actual fact-finding, writing reports, and holding press conferences. This infused a great deal of confidence in victims. In many places, people began reporting incidents and filing FIRs (first information reports). In 1985, when the Karamchedu massacre of Dalits happened, all democratic forces came together in a struggle—and he could mobilize their support. The challenge, however, was to sustain the mobilization and sustain the struggle. The formation of the DMS (Dalit Mahasabha) was a great event. Help arrived from all over the state, and Tharakam and his allies were able to build an organization of Dalits fighting for themselves. Tharakam resigned his post as a government pleader in 1985 in protest against the Karamchedu massacre, but he stayed in Karamchedu for a while. He was part of organizing the first all-India Dalit protest in Karamchedu.

Tharakam was the founding president of the AP DMS and continued in this position till 1991. He was the state convenor of the Chunduru Struggle Committee and in 1989 became the founding AP general secretary of the Bahujan Samaj Party (BSP). He resigned from the BSP in 1994, opposing its alliance with the Bhartiya Janata Party in Uttar Pradesh. Tharakam also was involved in the struggle against atrocities in other states—especially Karnataka and Bihar—and in 1987 organized an All India Dalit Writers' Conference. About a thousand writers attended, and the conference also featured several black writers.

Tharakam's first poetry collection, Nadiputtina Gontuka *(The Voice That Gave Birth to the River, 1983), was written in jail during the Emergency. A second collection,* Naalage Godavari *(The Godavari Is Like Me), came out in 2000. His booklet,* Poleesulu Arrestu Cheste *(If the Police Arrest You, 1979), was first published by APCLC and later serialized in the magazine* Commando. *It sold over 30,000 copies. The Hyderabad Book Trust republished it in 1983, and it ran for thirteen editions. Tharakam was interested in reading both Ambedkar and Marx. Under their influence, he wrote a book entitled* Kulam-Vargam *(Caste-Class, 1996). His other books include* Brazil Prajala Bhooporatam *(The Land Struggles of the Brazilian People, 2003);* Nela, Nagali, Moodeddulu *(Land, Plough and Three Oxen, 2008); and* Dalitulu-Rajyam *(Dalits and the State, 2008). His English writings include*

Constitution: Coup d'état *(2000). Tharakam translated important works by and on Ambedkar into Telugu before the Maharashtra government brought out the Ambedkar volumes. A founding trustee of Dr. B. R. Ambedkar Memorial Trust, set up in 1984 to disseminate Ambedkar's philosophy, he was also involved in the official project of translating Ambedkar's writings into Telugu. He was the coeditor for volumes one, four, and ten of these writings. He was editor of the Dalit little magazine* Nalupu *(1991–1994) and, since its foundation in 2008, of* Neeli Jenda *(Blue Flag, or Ambedkar's flag). A novel,* Panchatantram, *appeared in 2012, and a biography of his father entitled* Charitra Maarchina Manishi *(The Man Who Changed History) was published in 2016.*

Tharakam's novel Panchatantram, *excerpted here, portrays the life and conditions of the "untouchable" community (Malas) in coastal Andhra Pradesh. One of the protagonists, Sooranna, is a Mala person assigned the customary role of a "paaleru" (a farmhand) and subjected to inhuman and exploitative treatment. The novel is a story of the rise of an autonomous Adi-Andhra movement. In the novel, Tharakam pays his tributes to a well-known Dalit play titled "Paaleru" and depicts the social oppression and struggles of the Mala community between the 1940s and 1950s. Two excerpts from the novel are published here.*

The first excerpt presents the story of a romance between an upper-caste girl and a Dalit boy, Sooranna, a bonded laborer in the house of the village landlord. This relationship is against caste norms, and the landlord publicly burns the Dalit boy under the pretext that the boy had stolen valuable things from his house. The boy's family and the villagers "know" the truth but remain silent, as they also know the consequences.

The second excerpt emphasizes the significance of education in raising awareness about the injustices perpetuated by the dominant castes. It illustrates how education can bolster individuals' character, empowering them to combat oppression and pursue social mobility. Furthermore, it highlights the importance of solidarity and collective action in the quest for freedom. The enactment of the play "Paaleru" is central in this section, which also features a character named Sooranna, different from the Sooranna in the first excerpt.

Ammamma shouts, "Ey Lakshmi, he is milking the cow. Just keep a close watch over him."[1]

"Why, Ammamma? It is just routine work, isn't it?"

Ammamma slowly comes near Lakshmi and says, "It is not that. Your mother is not at home today; she went to attend the *bajana* at the temple.[2] By the time everyone finishes eating the *palaharam*,[3] the moon will have risen. You stand near the cow, because he is a useless thief."

"Ammamma, Sooranna is innocent, and not a thief. He is a nice person."

"What's 'nice?' Everyone is a good person as long as someone is watching. His father was also like him; he stole whatever he could get his hands on. Where do you think these qualities go?" says Ammamma.

Ammamma's husband is dead. She has been staying in her son-in-law's home for a long time. The son-in-law is her own brother's son. She also wants Lakshmi to get married to her son's son. If Lakshmi gets married to her grandson, then the dowry that was given for Lakshmi's mother will be returned to her home. However, if Lakshmi were to marry an outsider, then the property is lost. Most marriages are arranged in order to protect the families' property, which is probably why there is a proverb like "fight or marriage should happen with those of equal footing." Even though there are other equally powerful families like theirs, it is the thought of the loss of property that stops Ammamma from planning to wed Lakshmi into one of these families. Lakshmi is a single child who is the heir of immense wealth. In the surrounding area, Lakshmi's family are the landlords. When Lakshmi's grandfather died, her father did not even have an idea of where all they had properties. Any village they go to, it's their servants, agents, and their properties. All the relatives sat down and showed all the properties to Viswanatham in one go. He was shocked at his own properties. He kept saying, "I did not grow tall but drank the sky."

Everyone takes care of Lakshmi; moreover, her Ammamma pampers her a lot. Lakshmi's mother doesn't pay much attention to her, as her grandmother takes good care of her. Lakshmi's father does not care about anything other than looking after the properties, calculations, and their servants. He scares the servants and daily wage laborers, and once in a while, he beats them to death. If a servant passes away, he would give some money to the parents and ask them to burn the body near the water. He asks the parents to tell everyone that a snake bit the child. This is the way it has to happen and also the way it is happening.

---

[1]*Ammamma*—maternal grandmother.

[2]*Bajana*—any devotional song with a religious theme or spiritual ideas.

[3]*Palaharam*—snacks.

If a servant's father is seen bringing the dead body of his child from Viswananatham's field or compound, everyone knows it's because of "him." The whole village understands that it's Viswanatham's work if a parent says that a snake bit the child. No one talks about it nor informs Munsab.[4] Even if informed, it would be of no use. If someone somehow gathers the courage to speak to the officers, they end up getting beaten. Sometimes, the person would be made to disappear from the face of the Earth itself.

There is a flagpole in front of Munsab's home. They don't pray to it nor apply saffron or turmeric or tie neem leaves; it's the bonded laborers who are tied to the pole. They beat them up till death. However, the Munsab does not beat the bonded laborer to death, as he is well acquainted with the Sub Inspector of Police and the Tahsildar, which is the reason for him knowing how much to beat a person. It's not as if he is scared of the Tahsildar or the SI —why would he be? If a new recruit is appointed the SI or Tahsildar in his village, they visit him first. The police station itself is rented in his younger brother's house. The SI's house is in his brother-in-law's place. Then where can the SI go? He arranges for an amazing dinner right after the SI reaches the village.

The Munsab gets all the information about the SI—habits and interests, such as in women and playing cards. He finds out the SI's favorite food before he even arrives. On the first day, the SI is surprised to see all his favorite dishes already on his plate. He gets excited by seeing the beauty of the woman who is serving the food. He doesn't even check if there is a cot behind him—he just falls back along with her. Of course, there is alcohol at dinner. If there is no alcohol, then it is not dinner at all. And that's when all the *real* fun begins for the SI. No one would dare go against the Munsab when the situation is like this. They think it's enough if they are alive.

Viswanatham's and the Munsab's families have long-standing marital ties. Women from both sides have been marrying into each other's families since their grandfathers' time. Lakshmi's grandmother comes from one of these families. That is why Lakshmi's Ammamma lives with the confidence that her granddaughter won't marry outside these families. Whenever a marriage happens among them, it rarely goes beyond the next village. Everyone from these families is expected to stay visible to the elders. The elders must always be watching their actions and should know what is happening.

That is why, if any fights break out between these families, it is the elders who sort out the issues. Since everyone is related, one justifies the other person's mistake. If a mistake has happened in one family, the same mistake would have happened earlier in the other family or will happen for sure in the future. So, they nip the problem in the bud before it can become

---

[4]Munsab is a Telugu pronunciation of *munsiff*, which refers to a judge or magistrate.

serious. Especially if the conflict is related to wife-husband fights or property issues, it has to be sorted out. This has been a tradition from the start in these two families; that is *Kattadi.*[5] If anyone still continues to be the problem and has to be punished, eventually the other family members are to be punished. Both families make mistakes at some point or other, so they get adjusted to it. However, if a man has an extramarital affair (or multiple ones) or keeps a "second" home with another woman, it's not seen as a big crime. Strangely, even the women seem to adjust to it—maybe because they don't really have another choice.

If it is a woman from these families who is engaged in an extramarital relationship, it is ensured that this information doesn't leave the house. If the man belongs to another caste, and that too from a lower caste, the severity of the punishment changes based on the man's caste. In case the man is a servant of the family, then there is no mercy. The woman, however, will not be punished. It doesn't make any difference if a woman is married or not. If the relationship stops after the warning, the servant would be let off with a beating. On the off chance it continues, the servant would be killed, or else the servant's family would be asked to leave the village. Although the women are equally culpable, the punishment would only be given to the servant and his family. The servants do not dare to have relationships with the families of the landlords, as they know, after having seen so many dead bodies of their fellow men in front of their eyes, that they will be killed. However, when such extramarital relationships happen neither property nor caste comes in between, and there is not even fear of death.

Viswanatham had several extramarital relationships in the village. Lakshmi's mother did not approve of his behavior—she questioned it. The fights started two to three years after Lakshmi's birth. She threatened to go to her natal home if Viswanatham continued this behavior. She even went home once. The elders convinced her to change her mind, saying that such things happen. These things are normal to those two families. However, Lakshmi's mother could not adjust to it; she questioned him again. The elders sent her back to her family, hoping it would reduce the fights and that she would eventually adjust to the situation.

Initially, Viswanatham did not agree to let Lakshmi go to school. Even though the school was right next to the pond, just in front of their home, he was stubborn—he didn't want Lakshmi stepping out of the house. If necessary, he said, he would bring the teacher home. With that in mind, he gathered a group of children from his extended family and appointed a teacher to educate them at home. The other children eventually stopped coming, saying they wanted to go to school. Hearing their peers talk about the fun at school—playing, singing, all the excitement—they started craving that experience. There was no fun here, no such "happenings." Above all, the

[5]*Kattadi*—rules that are followed in the village to control a person or a family.

children were scared of Viswanatham. Eventually, Lakshmi too became stubborn about going to school and did not want to continue learning at home. When she wouldn't give in, Viswanatham reluctantly let her go—without conviction. For the first time, he was afraid of Lakshmi.

By the time Lakshmi finished her fifth class, a high school was introduced in their village. None of the surrounding villages had one, so many children were excited to join. Lakshmi was ready too.

She did not stop with fifth class, even though Viswanatham tried to discourage her. He kept saying that all kinds of "troublesome" people were enrolling, that it was a government school and not meant for "people like us." Every day, while others walked, Lakshmi went to school by vehicle—along with her four girl cousins. The boys rode bicycles. Many children traveled three to four miles from different villages just to attend school. Viswanatham often told her that all of them belonged to the lower caste. But Lakshmi did not understand any of it.

***

Lakshmi was not allowed to continue her education after high school. They decided to get her married. They did not need to look for any matches, as her mother-in-law's son, Gopalam, was already available as a groom. He was not literate, but no one saw that as a problem. Everyone said he didn't need an education—he had plenty of land. All he needed, they said, was to know how to do basic calculations.

Everyone in the family thought that if Lakshmi were to marry Gopalam, properties of both the families would be joined. But Lakshmi refused to marry Gopalam, citing his illiteracy. Nobody could convince her. She did not heed Viswanatham's menacing warnings nor Amma's threats of committing suicide. Everyone waited, thinking she would change her mind in a few days.

Ammamma shouted at Lakshmi, "When I ask you to go, why don't you?" Lakshmi flung open the main door and sat down on the doorstep. The night was thick with darkness, and a lone hurricane lantern lit the corner dimly. Just then, Sooranna arrived to milk the cow, and pulled the calf away from its mother.

Whenever Lakshmi's mother was not home, this duty of supervision fell upon Lakshmi. And every time she came for this duty, her interest increased. The calf—midway through drinking—would be pulled away, and the cow would be milked. After milking, the calf would be released from its separation from the mother. Again, the calf would start drinking milk. Probably the cow saved some milk to give to her child. Otherwise, how would any milk be available for the calf? Until Sooranna finished milking, the cow kept licking the calf. How mesmerizing! How absorbing! It was something Lakshmi saw regularly. Still, it looked different every day.

It was surprising how the milking of the cow seemed completely new to Lakshmi. The way Sooranna sat on his knees. The way he held the utensil with his knees. The cloth over his knees could not hold his muscles in place. The muscles shone under the lantern light. She felt as if the light was reflecting off black stone.

Milking is also an art! Not everyone can do that work. The cows also do not let everyone milk them. They only let someone they're familiar with touch their udders. If anyone else attempts to milk them, they would kick with their legs. Once in a while, if the usual person does not come to milk, there would be no milk at home that day, and they would have to go to their neighbor's home. In some homes, the wives would get used to milking a little bit. The cows would let the wife touch their udders. They do not let new people come near them. If a wife has to milk the cow, she struggles a lot. Even if Amma calls the neighborhood aunty, the cow won't listen to the aunty. Amma does not know how to milk the cow at all. It is very hard to tie the saree up to the waist in *gochi*[6] and kneel for a woman. The utensil placed between her knees would keep shifting. The women are used to tying their saree up while sprinkling water after sweeping the front yard. However, the women belonging to rich, upper-caste families and from Zamindars' households would never do such work, right? It's always the other women, the ones from lower castes, who tie their sarees at the waist. Whether they're working in the agricultural lands, sweeping, harvesting, or stepping into water, they always wear the saree that way. Everyone is a type. Their muscles are already tight from years of labor—and when they tie up the saree, the muscles tighten up even more.

Lakshmi was thinking about all these things. As Sooranna milked the cow, the sound—"Siiee, Siiee ..."—felt like music to her ears. She watched him switch hands, moving steadily over the udder, the rhythm almost calming.

As the milk utensil filled, the sound of milk sounded like the voice of a human. Once in a while, she wanted to shout to Soorana, "Orey! Do not milk it with so much force." She felt like his strong hands were touching her breasts. She even touched her breasts at times, imagining it was him.

In that way, with that scene of Sooranna milking the cow, desire blossomed in her heart. She could not understand how the cow was engrossed whether the calf was drinking milk or the farmhand was milking. How could the cow remain engrossed whether the calf was drinking or the farmhand was milking? Maybe the cow didn't realize he was taking the milk meant for her child. If she did, how could she let him? Maybe it was fear. Maybe they scared or beat her into it. That must be why she let them take her milk—afraid that if she didn't, they wouldn't let her calf drink at all. It's the same

---

[6]*Gochi*—loincloth, a traditional attire used by men.

with oxen. They're made to work through beatings. After a few lashes, they moved the cart, they plowed the field—without protest, without sound.

Lakshmi used to watch her father beat Sooranna when she was a child. Even for small mistakes, he would be thrashed. Sooranna was not allowed to run while getting beaten up. If he tried to escape, he'd be beaten even more. That was Viswanatham's rule. The beatings were not just for Sooranna but for his father as well. Even though Sooranna's father was older than Viswanatham, he still got beaten. Sooranna never saw his father questioning Viswanatham. He had seen the ox hiss, shake its horns, and refuse to move—but never once had he seen his father protesting this treatment. So what could Sooranna do when his own father never stood up? At times, Lakshmi used to think, "this servant's life is like that of the animals." What can she do?

Lakshmi had known Sooranna for as long as she could remember. He had been coming to the house with his father. Just like when an old ox dies and a new one is purchased, so too does Viswanatham get a new servant. Once in a while, Sooranna's mother would come to Viswanatham's home to take care of household work, and if there was no work there, then she would work in his field. The servants were paid in grains. If they asked, sometimes they were given a bit of money. Once the work in Viswanatham's fields was done, she would go to other farms as a daily-wage laborer. She and Sooranna lived on that money.

***

That's how Sooranna used to come along with his mother. Lakshmi's Ammamma said he was probably four or five years older than her. But in his height and build, he already looked just like his father. Ammamma never had a kind word for him. Amma used to give him leftover rice. They purchased a mud bowl for him. He had to eat from that mud bowl. No one else could touch it—not until all the utensils were washed.

Ammamma never let Lakshmi play with Sooranna, not even when she was little. If Lakshmi wanted to give him a toy, it had to be when Ammamma was not looking. If she saw, she would not beat her, but Sooranna. Although Lakshmi wanted to give him toys, she would not do so at the thought of getting him beaten up unnecessarily. And maybe, because of all those restrictions Ammamma placed on her, the desire only grew stronger—the urge to touch, to play, to run and jump with him. She would give him some food in secret, saying, "Eat quickly, otherwise Ammamma will see."

Slowly, without even realizing it, Lakshmi grew closer to Sooranna. She told herself it wasn't friendship. "Friendship with a servant? *Chii paadu ....*"[7] She convinced herself by thinking that this was her just showing a small

---

[7] *Chii paadu*—a term used to describe something bad.

mercy on someone who didn't have food to eat. The truth was that, without realizing it, she had become friends with Sooranna.

Sooranna did not have an idea about any of this. He never asked them for anything. He never asked Lakshmi for anything. His mother had told him never to ask for anything in the landlord's house. If they give something, take it and don't desire for anything that is in their home. "We won't get it, we are servants. If they give something, take it; but we should not ask for it. If you ask for anything, they will beat you." She reminds him, "Why get beatings?"

Viswanatham kept Sooranna to take care of the new cow. He wasn't allowed to ask for a salary—whatever Viswanatham gave, he had to accept. Sooranna's mother didn't have a say in this; she had to accept it. It was the best she could do. If she didn't agree, she would not get to live with her son. He would be working as a servant in some other village and be allowed to come home only once a year. The employment conditions remain the same in Malapeta, which is the reason she agreed to it without saying a word.

Sooranna had to come to Viswanatham's home early every morning. He would sweep the area where the cow was tied and carry the cow dung to the dungheap. Then he'd take the cow to the nearby pond and wait while it grazed on the grass. By afternoon, he'd bring the cow back, leave some grass for it to eat, and water to drink. If the landlord's family gave him food, he would eat it. Otherwise, he'd have whatever leftover rice was at home. But most days, there wasn't any food at home—if there wasn't enough for dinner, how could there be leftovers? In the evening, he'd repeat the same tasks—taking care of the cow. And like that, he grew up looking after the cow.

The nature of work changed based on his age, and so too did the working hours. There was not much difference to the salary, though. The work shifted from the house to the field. As Sooranna grew a little older, he was tasked with milking the cow at night. Once the milking was finished, he would do some other work before going home. Whenever the barbers came to massage Viswanatham's legs, they would walk back home together.

After the landlord's house, there were the homes of the washermen, barbers, and shepherds. Further down, after a long stretch, were the huts of Sooranna's community members. Unless the barber was scared or forced, he would never touch Sooranna. He shaved Viswanatham but never Sooranna. A member of Sooranna's own community had learned to shave and cut hair.

In this way, Sooranna's and Lakshmi's workloads grew so quickly as if they were the tallest building. The calf Sooranna had once tended to when he started his service with the landlord was now the same cow he was milking. That, in a way, was their relationship. The cow and its calf knew more about Sooranna than Lakshmi.

Sooranna would come to work before dawn and leave only after dusk. Lakshmi would see him working, but never as he entered or left the house. He ate his lunch at the landlord's home, but only after everyone else had finished. His food—some rice and curry—was brought to him at the entrance of the garden, which is where he had to eat it. There was even a separate plate just for him, in which his rice was served.

The cows would get their food, fermented cattle feed, in one big trough. Sooranna had a mud utensil, and if the utensil were broken, then there would be no food for that day. And until someone brought a utensil, he would not get his lunch.

In this way, he was raised in Viswanatham's yard. He was allowed near the veranda, the front platform, of the home only when he was needed. The front platform was tall and raised at both ends to resemble a throne. Sometimes, Viswanatham would sit there to rest. When visitors came, he would sit on that platform, and everyone else was expected to stand while talking to him. If the visitor was from Viswanatham's community, he was allowed to sit on the platform. But people like Sooranna, who worked as servants or daily wage laborers, were only allowed to stand away from the gate while remaining visible to Viswanatham. If Viswanatham couldn't hear what they were saying, he would scold them, "Will you die? Speak louder." Upon hearing scolding like this, they would half die, and whatever message they had to convey would be lost. They would stop this barrage of insults by saying *sittam babu.*[8] They often forgot why they had come.

Sooranna could only cross the threshold of the throne when absolutely necessary. He had no knowledge of what the house or its architecture looked like. It never even touched his thoughts.

***

One evening, Viswanatham and his wife, Parvathamma, went to a relative's wedding. Whenever Parvathamma went out, she used a bullock cart. They would tie the Mysore oxen to it—the very reason those oxen were purchased in the first place. They had been raised with great care. When the oxen were first brought home, the whole village came to see them. There was no comparison between the regular oxen and the Mysore ones. In height, physique, horns, and the way they walked and ran—they stood apart in every aspect. Even now, people from different villages would occasionally come just to catch a glimpse. Before setting out, the Mysore oxen would be tied to the cart, and a pooja would be done. As the cart passed through the village, people would come out of their homes to see the oxen. However, the cart itself was covered with veils at the front and back. No one could see who was sitting inside. It was tradition—for Parvathamma, for her mother, and for female ancestors as well.

Since they were attending a wedding, they took a washerman along. The cart driver was responsible for handling the Mysore oxen, while the

[8] *Sittam babu*—literally "as you wish sir," an expression of obedience to the upper-castes.

washerman looked after Viswanatham's needs. Viswanatham always needed a servant to shout "*Orey*" at. *Muhurtham* for the wedding was at midnight.[9] By the time all the rituals and changing of clothes were over, it would already be morning. However, the wedding would not happen in a day; it was a three-day wedding. At times, some have a five-day wedding. Relatives would travel from faraway places, meeting each other in the name of the wedding. These gatherings were rare, and no one could say when such joyful moments would come again. That's why, once they arrived, people stayed for four or five days, fully enjoying themselves. For women especially, those three days of wedding were a kind of freedom. They took charge of the work, gave orders, and did everything on their own terms. No one stopped them. No one questioned them.

People like Viswanatham would stay only one night, irrespective of how many days the wedding was planned for. Once in a while, Parvathamma would stay back for the rest of the celebrations. At times like this, it was Sooranna who guarded their home. He was asked to sleep just outside the house.

Sooranna finished all his work and that day was given food to eat at Lakshmi's home. Appalamma, who usually did the household chores, was also asked to stay the night. She was supposed to sleep in the company of Ammamma. Sooranna was asked to sleep outside the house. No one was expected to break in or steal anything—but his presence was meant as support for the women inside. That was all.

Sooranna fell asleep quickly. Once he was asleep, only his mother's voice in the morning could wake him. Lakshmi was asleep in her room. Ammamma and Appalamma were in another. Appalamma had a bedsheet; Sooranna had nothing. He spread out his head cloth at the edge of the house and lay down.

But Lakshmi could not sleep that night. No matter how hard she tried, her mind wouldn't rest. Her thoughts ran faster than the Mysore oxen. And just like the little bell tied around their necks, which tinkles, her desires in the heart too were making noise. She tried to catch those thoughts—but they slipped away, like a calf let loose.

It was too dark outside. But in her heart, she was lit by a thousand lamps, lightning, and thunder. Lakshmi and her thoughts were enough, and nothing else was visible to her. The house, and the people in it, slowly dissolved like smoke, shapeless and drifting. Even the glow of the lantern outside no longer reached her. She got up and stepped out slowly. She wasn't even aware she had opened the door to her room. It was like sleepwalking, as if her body moved on its own, without effort or intention. Usually, the door was difficult to open, but this time, she opened the door easily.

She called out to Sooranna in a low voice, "*Orey!*" He did not stir.

---

[9] *Muhurtham*—auspicious time.

She closed the main door and came out onto the verandah, and bending toward him, she called out "Sooranna." She thought she had called out to him, but maybe she hadn't—Sooranna didn't respond. He did not move. With her hand, she hit him softly, urging him to wake up.

He was startled awake and quickly sat up.

"Did you call me, *Chinnammagaru?*"[10]

"I am frightened," she said.

"What is there to fear, *Chinnammagaru?* My mother says the devils do not come when I am there."

"There is something moving around in my room; come and look," she said.

"Nothing will be there, *Chinnammagaru.* It is probably a cat. Wait. I will drive it out," replied Sooranna.

She walked back to her room, and he followed her.

It was his first time stepping into the courtyard!

"There is no noise anywhere; you just feared for nothing, *Chinnammagaru,*" he said.

"Don't talk loudly … Ammamma will wake up."

The lantern seemed to have dimmed as if on purpose—its faint light falling gently on her.

There was no top cloth on her body. Only a skirt and blouse.

It was Sooranna's first time seeing her so close.

He took a step as if to leave. She did not touch him but blocked the way with her hand.

"I'll go," he said. But he did not move.

She moved her hand forward a little and held his hand. She moved back a little. He only said, "*Chinnammagaru.*" She again moved forward a little. Holding his hand, she made a small opening in her blouse and put his hand on her breast and pressed hard. She did it thinking of the way Sooranna had milked the cow. Sooranna could not do anything. Her heart was pounding so loudly, it felt like the sound might escape her chest and echo outside.

With one of her hands, she removed her skirt. The skirt fell around her feet. He held both her hands and hugged her tight. That's it. How they slowly slipped to the ground … how their bodies leaned and collapsed into one another … how Sooranna moved over her like a boat tethered to the banks of the Godavari—she couldn't recall clearly. Like a crab emerging from the water, a heat rose and melted between them. She couldn't remember how Sooranna slipped into her, just like how water breaks through a barrier and rushes forward. It was an experience that words couldn't hold. The excitement lasted only a minute. That melting, that rush of water—flowing up and down—but for that one minute, how long had she waited? How many fears, how many worries, how much risk … and how fast it all happened.

---

[10]*Chinnammagaru*—a respectable word for a young girl of the family, literally "small madam."

Just like the Godavari slowing down, once their excitement settled, Sooranna got up. That was when he realized what he had done. Even though he kept telling himself he had only come because Chinnammagaru had called him, the fear was already gripping him. What if Peddammagaru had seen him? If the landlord came to know, there would be nothing but death for him! He stepped outside and sat down, as if he had lost everything. At that moment, he was too afraid to even glance back at the house.

Just to remember the happiness he had felt moments ago, he tried to reassure himself: "Who will know? Why be afraid? Chinnammagaru won't tell anyone." He didn't know when or how he fell asleep—he drifted off, still sitting.

***

Lakshmi did not appear before Sooranna for two days after the incident. Neither her mother nor grandmother had given her any tasks that would bring her into contact with him. However, it felt as though he was searching for her.

The fear of that first day was no longer present. Sooranna remembered a time when there was no fear at all—when he'd even climbed the coconut tree and drunk its water. He thought, when fear goes away, there's nothing you can't do.

On the third day after the incident, he was cutting fodder for the cows. As the sun was setting, the two cows—one currently a milk-giving cow, the other yet to give birth—had to be tied up at home. The cows took turns to provide milk for the household.

After cutting the fodder and tying up the cows, Sooranna noticed a vehicle approaching the field. It was common to see oxen carts coming to the farm, especially if the landlord was visiting. People would gather around the cart and build a temporary shade of date-palm leaves. But today, he was surprised—why was Lakshmi's mother coming at this time?

Lakshmi had convinced her mother to let her visit the field. Tomorrow was Ganesh Chaturthi, and she had asked her for permission to fetch lotus flowers.

They had a big pond on their farm.

The pond was filled with lotuses.

No children were allowed to touch or pick those flowers; sometimes, they would steal them though. Even for festivals, her mother would usually say, "Sooranna will bring them. Why should you go?"

But today, Lakshmi insisted, "He won't know which ones, Amma. If I go, I can choose the ones that are fully bloomed, with bright colors. He will just pluck buds and bring them."

"Fine, it's your wish. Go, and return quickly." Lakshmi immediately left for the farmland.

Appanna stopped the bullock cart by the field and helped her down. From a distance, hidden behind the trees, Sooranna watched. The farm had a few rooms: a couple of rooms in varying sizes for the animals, one for storing coconuts, and a resting room for Viswanatham at the far corner. He would use this room during his daytime visits to the farm, and sometimes he also brought women there. No one asked questions. No one dared to. That's how the people around the field lived their lives.

There was about a mile between the village and the field. Abruptly, Appanna remembered some urgent work that he had to do and asked Lakshmi for permission to quickly head back to the village. He requested her to pluck the flowers by the time he was back. He told one of the other laborers to pluck custard apples and rushed off. Then, Sooranna entered.

From that moment till now, the only thing Lakshmi had uttered was, "*Orey*, pluck the lotus flowers and bring them back."

He dropped the pile of fodder without a word and started walking toward the pond. She followed him.

She stood on the cement steps to the pond. Sooranna stepped into the pond, wearing nothing but a thin cloth tied around his waist—shorter than a towel.

"That flower … not that … ahh, that red one," she called, pointing and making him wade all around the pond.

The water reached up to his chest.

Holding a handful of lotus flowers, Sooranna swam toward the edge, pushing the lotus leaves out of his way.

"Bring what you've plucked," she said.

Sooranna gave her whatever was in his hand. "Bring more," she ordered, sending him back into the water.

Lakshmi walked toward the animal shed, carrying the flowers. The room where her father usually stayed was locked. Sooranna followed her with another handful of lotus blooms.

In the shed, there was a pit for storing grass, and it was filled with dried grass.

She asked him to pile up all the lotus flowers.

The water on Sooranna's body had not yet dried. He did not have another cloth to wipe it off.

If Lakshmi hadn't been there, he would've dried himself off and tied the same wet cloth again around his waist. But with her standing there, he had no chance to do that and stood in his damp cloth.

"Not one bunch, two," she said, asking him to tie the flowers together. And, slowly, she held his hand and led him toward the far end of the hay. He had thought he would have to hold her tightly so she wouldn't run—but she was the one who led him.

Once again, full concentration. Another intercourse.

Though it was new, it felt familiar. And yet, though familiar, it felt entirely new.

***

No matter how many experiences follow, the first one always remains unforgettable. Everything after that feels like a flood—rushing, fleeting, overwhelming.

It did not take long for Parvathamma to figure out that Lakshmi was pregnant. Just by observing her behavior—especially the way she vomited twice every morning right after waking up—she grew anxious. Lakshmi herself was unaware. She noticed the vomiting but had no idea why it was happening.

Parvathamma, on the other hand, understood what it meant, and the realization left her shaken. She asked Lakshmi what had happened.

Lakshmi behaved as if she knew nothing.

On top of that, she gave a counter question: "What happened?"

"What happened?! You got pregnant without getting married—that's what happened," Parvathamma snapped in anger.

Lakshmi was surprised. She couldn't believe what she was hearing. *We didn't even meet more than twice*, she told herself.

"With whom?" Parvathamma demanded.

Gopalam might have come when she was not there; if someone had come, it must be him, Parvathamma thought. That would've been easier—if it was Gopalam, Amma wouldn't have said anything. But he had stopped coming around. He was angry, hurt even, because Lakshmi had refused to speak to him in a friendly manner.

Parvathamma was sure it wasn't him. "Is it Gopalam?" she asked again.

Lakshmi stayed silent.

"Your father will kill you if you do not answer. If it's Gopalam, then there is no issue. We will get you married."

At this, Lakshmi was somehow able to say, "It is not him." But how could she say it was Sooranna? She was terrified they would kill him.

Finally, Parvathamma understood. She broke down, crying without stopping. "You took away our honor, bitch," she screamed, striking Lakshmi in a storm of rage and whirlwind of emotions. It was the first time she had ever hit her.

That night, Parvathamma told Viswanatham. He flew into a rage. He called Lakshmi and beat her severely—it was the first time he had ever raised a hand against her. He used to call Lakshmi "Amma." He would introduce Lakshmi to everyone as his mother. Everyone thought that she looked like her grandmother. They had even given her the same name. Viswanatham felt proud watching Lakshmi wear her grandmother's jewelry and walk around the house. And yet, that night, his anger was uncontrollable as he continued hitting her. Lakshmi did not say a word. She bore everything in silence. She cried through the night. Viswanatham and Parvathamma couldn't sleep either.

Parvathamma told her mother the next morning. Her mother collapsed to the ground when she heard the news. Lakshmi never told her it was Sooranna.

They sent a vehicle to bring the doctor. He was an Ayurvedic practitioner.

"There is nothing to be worried about," said the doctor, and he went away after treating Lakshmi.

***

Sooranna came to work as usual the next morning. As he was washing the cow, Viswanatham appeared, hurling abusive words. Without warning, he grabbed a thick rope and struck Sooranna. For the first time, Sooranna ran. He had never done that before—no matter how harsh the beatings, he would stand still and take it. But not today. Today, he ran. Today, he didn't want those beatings. Viswanatham chased him down, caught him, and tied him with a rope before continuing the beating. Parvathamma watched from inside the house. Lakshmi had had a dream of a bull attacking Sooranna. When she woke, she could hear Sooranna's cries of pain. She saw it all happening from her room. It was more than she could have imagined; she was afraid. Viswanatham hit Sooranna until he was tired and then called his laborers.

"Tie him to the temple pole. Call the pandit, and ask him to do the ritual."

They untied Sooranna and took him to the temple. At the temple stood a large wooden pole that had been there since time immemorial. It is to this pole that the people who are to be punished are tied up and beaten. They are punished according to the elders' wishes. Some are beaten with sticks, others with whips. A few have hot iron rods pressed into their flesh. Some lose teeth. Others are doused in kerosene and set alight.

It happens in this place; that's it. No one should talk about it anywhere else. They are not to discuss it with anyone.

The laborers brought Sooranna to the pole. It was still early morning; the temple grounds were empty. The only house nearby belonged to the priest—a modest structure built for him when the temple was established. He lived there with his wife and son, brought from elsewhere to serve this temple. The priest was allotted two acres of temple land. He had leased it out for cultivation. But Viswanatham claimed it as his own—a "donation" to the temple from his family. Only Viswanatham, Karanam and Munsab knew the truth: it was government land. Years ago, during Viswanatham's father's time, the government handed out land to anyone willing to cultivate it. Later, documents were drawn, and land boundaries shifted quietly into Viswanatham's growing estate. He then allowed others to work the land near the pond.

"Why give the land for lease? I shall cultivate it and give you some grains every year," Viswanatham told the priest. The priest also believed it was Viswanatham's land.

And that is why the priest obeyed anything Viswanatham said. Long ago, he had declared that burning alive by tying to a pole as a punishment is as per the Shastras. There was no opposition. As always, Munsab was intimidated into silence.

The laborer asked Sooranna, "Did you steal the utensils?"

"I did not," replied Sooranna. He did not have the energy to answer loudly, as he had been beaten up badly.

The priest lit the camphor at the temple.

He asked Sooranna to hold out his right hand.

Sooranna did as he was told. Before placing the camphor, the priest declared, "This flame will be set on your right palm. If your hand remains unburnt, then you are innocent. But if you feel pain—if your skin burns—then you have stolen. Think carefully. You are standing before God. Do not lie."

"God will be watching all this. If you haven't lied, then God will take away the fire. If you are lying, even if the fire seems fine, God will punish you. Think about it," warned the priest.

By then, a crowd had gathered near the temple. Must be a big theft. "Otherwise, why such a severe punishment?" thought everyone who came there. No one there felt what was happening was wrong or a grave injustice.

Everyone in the village used the same pond, built with neat cement steps. Upper-castes never fetched water themselves—their farm laborers did. Those farm laborers, even if just for a moment, felt like they belonged to the higher caste. Other castes collected water from farther down. However, untouchables never came to this pond. Their houses weren't even in the village. Moolapalli was a mile away. No one from there knew what was unfolding at the temple that morning. And no one went to tell them.

The priest asked him thrice, but no matter how many times he was asked, Sooranna's answer remained the same. The priest called for the washerman to come to the temple. He asked the washerman to hold the lit camphor. Sooranna was unaware of the illusion that was being staged in front of him. Sooranna thought, I didn't steal anything—why would my hand burn?, and it gave him courage.

The burning camphor was placed on Sooranna's hand. The crowd watched. Some young men stepped closer to Sooranna. The priest knew what would happen. He stepped back. Sooranna's right palm was burnt.

"Thief! Thief!" everyone shouted.

"Got caught," said someone.

"Where will he go?" asked another.

"This wouldn't happen unless God allows it," said an old man.

Saying such things, a few people left.

"Thief! Rascal!" some yelled, and began to beat him with sticks.

Sooranna could not understand how all of this was happening. He looked at everyone as if they were crazy.

"I don't know anything. I did not steal anything. Did not," Sooranna kept repeating.

No one listened, and no one would.

"What are you waiting for? Set him on fire," clamored the crowd, while abusing him with swear words. Listening to them, one of the farm laborers brought a kerosene bottle. They poured the kerosene over his head and spread it all over his body. They checked to see whether he was fully doused in petrol. One of them lit a matchstick, and Sooranna was no longer visible. There was only fire—blazing from a red body. Once the whole body was on fire, everyone left.

Only then did the news reach Sooranna's home.

Viswanatham felt nothing about burning Sooranna alive. He went to Munsab's place. He sat down at the entrance to his compound. Munsab already knew what had happened, without Viswanatham saying anything.

Munsab was silent for a while.

"Ask his father to come and collect his body."

This was how Sooranna's family got to know.

The moment Sooranna's family heard the news, the young and the old ran toward the village.

Everyone stood in silence, stunned by what had happened.

The body was fully burned, with an odor surrounding the place.

At first, a shiver ran through them.

Who would ask about what happened? Who could ask?

Sooranna was a farm laborer, and so was his father. How would they ask? Where was the courage?

They were sure that Sooranna had not stolen anything. Sooranna's father, elder Sooranna, did not dare to ask. But his mother could not hold back.

She wept aloud, crying that her son had been beaten and killed. She wanted to know the truth.

When she tried to touch her son, other women stopped her.

"I will go and ask," she told her husband.

"No. He is not a good man. The one who is gone won't return. Our luck is not good, so don't ask."

Sooranna's mother refused. She stood firm. "I will go," she said—and began to walk.

Viswanatham was sitting on the front platform of his house. Even when he was home, he often sat there for long hours. Only men from his caste were allowed to sit beside him. Others had to stand outside. If it's someone like Sooranna's father, they definitely had to stand outside and wait until he called. He would call them whenever he pleased. They had to remain outside the gate, with folded hands. There was no question of women stepping forward and speaking. Usually, there would be one or two people sitting across from Viswanatham on a bench. But there was no one that day. One or two young people would get off their bicycles and start walking when they reached Viswanatham's house. Panchama children were not allowed to ride bicycles in front of him.[11] They were not supposed to wear slippers either. If a girl was seen riding a bicycle and the people sitting on the bench recognized her, they would not say anything to the girl—but her father would be summoned and yelled at or punished. Eventually, the father would instruct her to behave in a certain way.

However, this time, unlike every other time, Sooranna's mother did not stop at the corner of the gate. She stood right in front of the gate.

"Lord, why did you kill my son? Even if he had stolen something, you could have let him off with a few smacks. But to burn him alive? Is that why I kept him here, to work for you?" she said, pausing again and again through her crying.

"Will we kiss the person who steals from us?"

Before she could say something, Viswanatham cut her off with, "He did steal, and it has been proven. We placed camphor on his palm, and it burned. I asked him myself—he lied and said he didn't take anything. He got what he deserved."

Sooranna's father knew his son did not steal. His mother knew, and so did everyone else.

Sooranna's mother looked up at him—frail, tired, her body aching with grief. "Whatever you say, Lord, I know one thing: my son would never steal. If he did anything stupid, you should have scolded him, beaten him—we wouldn't have said anything. Aren't landlords here to teach our children values? My son did not steal," she wept.

A couple of people chimed in with, "Yes, sir. He was a nice person."

"Those immature sons of bitches. Who will listen to you? You're all so virtuous, are you? Then why are coconuts disappearing from the canal's edge? The SI keeps asking me to file a complaint—I've kept quiet. One word from me and you boys will be behind bars. Go away before I do something about you people," he shouted, swearing at them.

The boys stood silent. Their only courage was in asking about Sooranna. No one had dared even that much before.

"Orey, come here!" Viswanatham called Sooranna's father and flung a hundred rupees' worth of loose change at his face. Then he asked him to finish the funeral rituals before sunset.

"No need, Lord. Keep your hundred rupees. Our hands are not broken—we will bury our son ourselves. I raised him with these hands. If I must dig his grave, so be it. This is our life," Sooranna's mother said, in between tears.

---

[11]*Panchama* is a term used to refer to Dalit communities in colonial India.

"Why, Lord? Why should people like us live? You have killed your laborer and me as well. You have thrown all of us into the pond." She continued speaking like this amid her weeping.

They didn't know what they were saying or doing—such is the state when someone cries beyond their own consciousness, when grief boils into uncontrollable agitation. Like a calf snapping its rope and running wild, she began to shout words no one had dared to utter. Whether anyone else heard or not, Viswanatham heard them loud and clear.

"How many people will the landlords kill? Someone will come and see your cruelty. How long? How many days will this go on?" Viswanatham could not believe what he was hearing. Not just he; everyone in the village who heard these words felt the same. He reached for his stick, fuming: how dare this bitch, the wife of his laborer, speak in such a loud and bold voice?! That too on his doorstep!

"Please stop!" someone shouted from inside the house.

Viswanatham was shocked. Whenever he spoke to anyone outside the house, his wife had never stepped out nor said anything. If there was any emergency, she would ask one of the laborers to inform him. She had never called out, let alone in a voice loud enough for ten people to hear. "She is crying for her son. Why are you going at her again?" Parvathamma asked.

Viswanatham felt like beating his wife with the stick. He did not know what to do. He had never had to control his rage, and he had never brought down his stick without beating anyone. This was the first time it had happened. No one had questioned his authority before. "Go away, bitches. Die!" shouted Viswanatham, and he stormed off in the direction of Munsab's house.

The people of Sooranna's community didn't know he had gone there. When they arrived, they saw the two men—Viswanatham and Munsab—sitting together. The people felt helpless when they saw them together and told each other, "What could we possibly tell Munsab now?"

Munsab asked the village servant to move the chair for Viswanatham. After doing as instructed, the village servant stood silently, facing the village.

He was not supposed to listen to what they were saying. And even if he did hear their words, he was expected to forget them immediately. Still, memories stuck with him, and he often found it hard to detach himself from the village's problems.

The servant and Sooranna belonged to the same caste—they were neighbors and even relatives. When he saw Sooranna's mother approaching, he was taken aback. He already knew what had happened. He had seen Sooranna's body. But to see all of them coming to Munsab's house like this—it was unheard of. He stopped them at the gate and informed them that the landlord was already inside.

At times, the servant behaved as if he were Munsab himself, relaying messages on his behalf, acting like he was in charge.

"Why have they come? Go ask them," said Munsab.

"They came to talk about Sooranna," the servant replied. Before he could say anything more, Munsab yelled, "What is there to talk about? Ask them to leave!"

"My son did not just die, Lord. He did not steal anything. They burned him alive!" shouted Aademma. Her voice sounded like a mix of lightning and thunder.

"Who would kill him? You asked him to steal, and now you act innocent. Go, go," screamed Munsab.

"Not like that, sir," a young man tried to explain.

"Who is that?" Munsab asked.

"He is the son of a military man's brother," answered the servant.

"He filed a complaint against you the day before yesterday," Munsab said. "Let's see who else is with you. We'll write complaints against all of you and hand them to the Head Constable. Their madness will vanish once they see what law means. I've been silent only because we all belong to the same village. But they're crossing the line now."

"Come here," Munsab called to the village servant.

Munsab made it sound like there was nothing more to be done. Everyone left without saying a word.

Munsab wasn't just a man who filed cases. He was known to beat people himself or have others beat them on his word. He could twist a false case into a punishment. He bargained over bail money and bribes—"from the highest to the lowest, everyone has to be paid," he often said. "It's not all for me."

The boys realized it was no longer safe to linger there and left, taking Sooranna's mother with them. With the small crowd that had gathered, they wrapped Sooranna's burnt body in a torn bed sheet, placed it on their shoulders, and took him to Malapeta, the residential area of Malas.

***

Sooranna's mother went back as there was nothing she could do. They prepared the funeral rituals. They laid down the body, and four people stood to each side of the bed and took the body toward the drainage canal.

Sooranna's mother cried continuously.

She was remembering his childhood and weeping. "You did that … you were like that, son. God has taken you away so quickly. Such a sinner I am; he did not take me. What did you do wrong?" she continued crying. There was no sense in the few words she was saying.

They didn't have a cemetery. So, they buried Sooranna at the end of Malapeta, near the drainage canal. If someone had the ability, they would build a pyre. Sometimes, they found bones when they dug. They placed the body where someone else was already buried. They buried Sooranna and washed their hands and legs in that same drainage canal before going back home.

***

Elder Sooranna stopped talking after Sooranna's death. It was not novel for them to be killed by landlords, but the death of his child was too much to handle. He didn't know what to do. The landlords ensured that they never thought about anything. If they started thinking, then they would have to be considered humans. And if that were the case, then everyone would become equal. A landlord would be human, and so would be the laborer. How could this happen?! A landlord is a landlord, and a farm laborer is only a laborer. There is a difference between the two, and there always is to be. Such is their life. Like a sparkle in the darkness, he remembered something.

The village servant had mentioned it—a small group of around ten people had gathered beneath the peepal tree by the canal, talking among themselves. That very day, a British lord was to pass through, on his way to the lighthouse at Munipalem. For this journey, the lord and his convoy had to cross Sooranna's Malapeta. There were a few people sitting near the peepal tree to catch a glimpse of a British lord; others went to the fields to try their luck.

The postman who delivered letters to the British lord lived in the next village. He passed through Sooranna's Malapeta once a week. He would gather a week's worth of letters and hand them over all at once. From the post office to the lighthouse, it was a five-mile stretch.

The postman paused when he saw the people near the peepal tree. He waited to say hello to elder Sooranna. While talking to elder Sooranna, he mentioned something the British lord always told them. "If we face any injustice, we should talk to a higher-order officer. If we just sit in fear, we will achieve nothing."

The lord always came to the weekly market yard with a village servant. The servant would hold a steel rod, which would be used to tap rhythmically against the ground as he walked ahead of the British lord. Even if he were burdened with packages from the market, he would never stop making the sound.

Near the lighthouse, only white men were visible.

"Only the white man knows that kind of magic! To light up the lighthouse, to put the light out—and see how far the light stretches into the sea. Then again, the light reflects back onto the coconut trees near the pond."

By now, the British lord would have gone far ahead. But the postman's words stayed with Sooranna's father. The clanging of the steel rod was resounding in his ears.

That night, when the village servant returned from work, elder Sooranna went to meet him.

"What do I do? I am unable to think of anything apart from my Sooranna's incident," he said.

"What will you do? What can people like us do? It is an issue with the landlord. How can we handle something like that? Leave it. You buried him. Let the soil take it all. Is this a new thing for us?" responded the village servant.

"No, uncle. I am certain that Sooranna was killed by Viswanatham. You saw the marks on his body, right? The story about stealing, hand-burning, and everything is a drama. My heart can't accept any of this, uncle. I know you will say the dead don't come back. Then you'll ask what I or the rest of us can do when he doesn't return, and that nothing is in our hands. And we can never beat the landlord. How, uncle? You are the one who knows everything; if you yourself say this, then what do we do? Your daughter is suffering because of the memories of her son. She keeps saying there's no reason to live when he is dead. We will die too. What do we have to be alive for? And it's not because of all she has been saying. You think of justice. You know everything, right? You work for Munsab, you go to Karanam, you talk to RI,[12] you go to the Tehsildar, and you go to court and give witness statements. Is there anything you do not know, uncle? If you think, there will be a way for us. As for me, I feel like telling the Tehsildar. He might do something. If not, we will leave. Please help with this one thing. Not for me, but for the one who is dead. For the injustice that happened to him." He said all of this in one go.

The village servant was shocked. Was this really Sooranna's father?! Was it he who uttered these words?!

The village servant knew what it meant to inform the Tehsildar. He knew what happened to the ones who went to the police with complaints against landlords. Their bodies were later found floating in the Godavari. Or found in bushes, with vultures eating them.

If they even suspected the village servant of being part of this, he would lose his job immediately. And if that happened—how would he survive? He couldn't plow the land like the others. He couldn't lift and weigh the grain sacks anymore.

"Orey, I fold my hands before you even though you are younger to me. Please leave me—not just me; please just do not think of this at all. It's not for people like us. Our fathers never did such things," he told elder Sooranna. He added, "If anything were to happen, don't let my name come out." Elder Sooranna replied, "Okay uncle. I will do whatever I can."

Elder Sooranna returned home. Since Sooranna's death, he hadn't gone back to work. Aademma was also at home. He sat in front of their home,

---

[12]RI refers to Revenue Inspector.

thinking. He shared his thoughts with his wife. At first, she was scared, but later she agreed. Her fear of what would happen to her husband if he went ahead with what he planned made her want to join him. Fear meant she was scared something would happen to her husband, so that was the reason she wanted to join him.

"Why would you come? Women should not go to offices; I will go and be back," he told Aademma.

"Then, take Venkanna." Venkkanna was her brother's son.

"No need. Why him? It will end up as a rope around his neck. I shall go."

She remembered how her husband did not say a word before Munsab. She believed if someone went with him, he would have some support. But he would not listen and wanted to leave before sunrise. He said, "Don't tell anyone about this."

Late that night, the village servant came by elder Sooranna's home. The village servant felt there was something he could do about the incident. But he came as if it were an ordinary visit.

He sat outside and asked, "Did you eat anything?"

"Ah, we shall eat," Aademma replied from inside.

Her sister-in-law was sending over whatever she was able to cook. They were eating morning's food at night and night's food in the morning.

"What curry did your sister-in-law send?" the village servant asked, in an attempt to shift the conversation. Part of him wanted to talk about Sooranna; the other part just wanted to give their minds a break.

"I did not check," she said. The village servant was a close relative of Aademma's father. In that village, everyone was related in some way or another. The bonds they had were thick. No one was a stranger there. In pain, everyone was there to help, save, and give a hand to each other. When someone died, it felt like a death in every home, and they did all that needed to be done.

Aademma brought the lantern close to the curry pot and said, "It's dried prawn curry."

"Bring me two prawns—my mouth feels nothing."

Elder Sooranna hadn't spoken a word till then. It was the village servant who kept the conversation alive, speaking now and then with Aademma. After a while, he turned to elder Sooranna and said, "I am going. I have to weigh the washerman's clothes in the morning."

The village servant was certain that elder Sooranna would definitely go to Munivaram. He had been thinking that the moment he left home. Then, he even thought of informing Munsab. And then changed his mind, thinking he might be of no help. After all, he did not take elder Sooranna to the Tahsildar. If word got out, they wouldn't even leave a body behind. They would beat him, toss him into the canal, and by morning he'd be floating out into the sea.

For some reason, he couldn't bring himself to stop the man. He too believed Sooranna had been killed for no reason. Viswanatham had done it willfully.

Viswanatham and Munsab were relatives—what could people like the village servant do? He had witnessed everything. He knew how many the landlords had killed—no one ever dared to complain. If other people fought among themselves and were not listening to the landlords, then the landlords would complain against them. Apart from them, it was the families of the dead and those who were killed who would come to Munsab. He convinced them. Sometimes, even if an FIR was registered, Munsab would bribe the SI and tear up the FIR, thus forcing a settlement between the two parties. Sooranna's incident was different. It was the landlord who killed him. And who would an FIR be filed against then? Even then, elder Sooranna was spirited about it and was determined: whatever happened, he would go to meet the Tahsildar. That night, the village servant came to offer at least some words of support—if nothing else.

As he stood up to leave, he said, "My advice—don't go. But if you must, go early. You'll reach by the time the office opens." He pressed a five-rupee note into his hand.

It wasn't the money that gave elder Sooranna strength—it was the words, "go early."

Before the first cock crowed, elder Sooranna set off for Munivaram.

Aademma woke up at midnight. She desperately wanted to go with him, but he wouldn't allow it. There was still some rice left, so she had cooked it before sleeping. She let it cool and cut a fresh banana leaf in the dark. She scooped the rice and curry onto it, tied the bundle tight, and wrapped it all in a cloth.

"After getting down in Munivaram, eat this food and then go to the office. We don't know when the work will conclude successfully," said Aademma.

"I'll get the work done even if I have to stay there for two nights," said Sooranna's father. As decided, he left by the first bus. By the time he got on, the bus was half full, and no one he knew was on the bus.

***

He looked around after getting off the bus in Munivaram. Though he had been to the town two or three times before, he had never come alone. He didn't know the way to the Tahsildar's office.

"It's in a two-story building," is what the village servant had told him.

Near the big canal, midway between the two bridges, stood all the offices. He reached the Tahsildar's office by asking people along the way. The food parcel was still on his shoulder. He did not feel like opening it. He was not hungry. The Tahsildar's office was made of stone. He couldn't figure out where to go or whom to ask. The compound was wide, with big trees around it.

He looked around. Some people were sitting under the trees, doing some work, and talking. A few were going in and out of the building. Some came back from inside and handed papers to the ones sitting under the trees. After taking the papers that were given out from a bag, they hurried inside.

Under one tree, a woman sat who looked like Aademma. A young boy was with her. "Might be her son," thought elder Sooranna.

He gathered his courage and walked up to the boy and told him what he had come for.

"It is hard," said the boy.

"I still want to speak about my pain," said elder Sooranna.

"There—see that teacher under the tree, wearing a red lungi and writing something—go to him. He will write a letter for you. You can give it to the Tahsildar," the boy advised.

Elder Sooranna felt encouraged and walked quickly. He felt so happy thinking that he was going to meet the Tahsildar.

The teacher was writing something as another person spoke. He read aloud what he was writing. When he finished with two or three other people, he looked at elder Sooranna and made a hand gesture, asking why he had come. Before he could reply, the teacher dipped his pen in ink and asked, "Which village are you from?" He did not sound like he did when he spoke to the others.

Elder Sooranna stood a little distance away. He wondered if the teacher looked at him differently, noticing the new lungi tied to the knees and the one-piece chest cloth. Still, he spoke firmly and explained the reason he had come.

After listening, the teacher wrote something down. He asked for a thumb impression. Once done, he told him to go up the steps and hand the paper to the Tahsildar.

As he was about to leave, he asked elder Sooranna for fifty paise.

Elder Sooranna pulled out the money from his chest cloth, gave the exact amount, folded his hands, and walked away.

He reached the hall shown to him. There, a peon was sitting at a big table. The man's attire made elder Sooranna nervous; he couldn't take a step forward. A red cloth was tied around his waist, another was draped across his shoulder, and a cap sat firmly on his head. Seeing all this, elder Sooranna felt as if he were the Tahsildar himself.

The peon wasn't letting anyone inside. He watched everything, decided who could go, and handled it all. When landlords arrived, he stood up, folded his hands, and led them either to the Tahsildar's room or somewhere else, depending on their business. When he noticed elder Sooranna, he barked, "Move aside!"

Elder Sooranna had tied his food parcel that he had brought with him from home to a tree branch. Holding the paper close to his chest with folded hands, he stood in one position.

For a long time, the peon didn't speak to him. Each time their eyes met, Elder Sooranna would bow to him. Only after a long while did the peon finally gesture for him to come. He went up the stairs. "What is that?" the peon asked him. He gave him the paper.

Elder Sooranna believed he had read everything in the paper. "Oh, a lot of such things are being brought to us. Who's going to look into this? You think the Tahsildar has no other work?" the peon shouted.

"My son was killed," said elder Sooranna.

"It won't happen. See that man sitting in the front yard? Give it to him and leave. Tahsildar won't look at it," the peon replied.

Elder Sooranna took the paper and gave it to the person in the yard.

The man glanced at him, stamped the paper without a word, and asked him to leave. He wondered why people like elder Sooranna came to the Tahsildar's office.

Still, elder Sooranna felt as though he had told everything to the Tahsildar himself and shared his pain. As if his son had gotten justice. He bowed respectfully to the men in the yard and to the peon, then began walking home.

He went back to the tree where he'd tied the food parcel. He took it down, carried it to the canal, washed his feet and face, and sat under the same tree. He believed the work had been done by submitting the paper.

There was a last bus that stopped in their village. The next morning, it would start as the first bus from their village.

While on the bus, he went over all that had happened. Suddenly, he cried out, "My head is broken, Amma!" By the time he could move back, two others had already hit him with a stick. With those blows, he fell down. The three people, who beat him up, threw him into a narrow canal.

At home, Aademma didn't expect him back that night, as he'd told her he wouldn't return until the work was done.

The next day, when one of the laborers was going to work, he saw a body in the canal. He went closer and saw that it was elder Sooranna. He ran to give the news to the people in the Malapeta. The village servant was informed too. Half of Malapeta went along with him. When they reached the canal, they saw that it was indeed elder Sooranna.

The young and the old came to the canal. *It hadn't even been a week since the son died. Now the father, too,* thought everyone with surprise. It was normal to be killed by landlords and be buried near the sewer.

We will never know how Aademma could handle seeing the dead body of her husband. She looked at everyone with crazed eyes. She didn't cry or utter a word. "Only I am left. Kill me as well. We are your farm laborers. We broke our backs working for you. Kill us for that, sir. Kill us!" was all that she said.

With the end-term exams about a month away, teachers began keeping students back for an extra two hours after school. One teacher, Veerraju, had bought a big lamp to help them study in the evenings. He would always be available to the students for any academic doubts they had. He started paying special attention to Sooranna.

He spoke to Sooranna's grandmother and made an arrangement. He would bring her enough groceries for a month, and she would cook for him. When he offered to pay her, she refused. She said she would cook but didn't want any money.

"If you don't take it, I won't eat," Veerraju said. Unable to give a good answer, she agreed. Veerraju asked Sooranna to eat with him. He would share some of his own food with the boy. At night, Aademma would make a full plate of food and leave it at Veerraju's house.

Veerraju slowly became part of the village. Sooranna felt stronger with him around. Veerraju prepared all the Malapeta students for their exams. They would gather at his home and study together. It felt like a big event for them.

Earlier, if ten people gathered in this manner, it would only be for bajana. They would sing devotional songs till early morning and then go home. Some would go straight to their farms from there. But now, those bajana gatherings stopped.

There was a small temple in the middle of Malapeta. It was built like a room but open on three sides, with a wall on the fourth side. Veerraju master started making the children study there.

Everyone would walk to high school together. On the way, the master would talk to them about many things. They felt as if they were in another world. He taught them new games, songs, and words.

As the exams got closer, he stopped the children from playing and made them focus on their studies.

Sooranna and his classmates had to go to another school to write the exams. Subbarao took them to Munivaram. There, they went to a postmaster's home. After listening to everything, the postmaster asked them to stay at his place.

"I too studied the same way. I was the only one in my village. There was no one to help me out. There was no one who was educated either. You're lucky—at least five of you are writing your final exams, and Subbarao is helping. It was all fear when I was studying! I never knew who would beat or scold me. Till the last day, I wasn't sure they would even let me sit for the exam. The Headmaster told me before the exam date that the hall ticket had arrived. Luckily, my paternal aunt lived in that village. After reaching there, I went out early in the morning, found the exam center, and wrote the exam on my own. I worked so hard, but still—there was no other way. It's all right, write the exam well … write and go to college. Don't stop with this," the postmaster said. They had brought rice, enough for that night. It would last them through the day. "Tomorrow, after the exam, you can eat at the hotel nearby," he told them.

For these kids, it was all a new experience—one they had to figure out on their own. Subbarao thought, *once they go through this themselves, it'll leave a deep impact on the way they think.*

During the summer holidays, the school-going children would also go to work as coolies. Similarly, during the school term, on holidays and Sundays, they would go for whatever work was available. Sometimes they even took leave from school to earn a little. The money saved would go into buying new clothes or school books.

But Sooranna's grandmother never let him go for manual work. "As long as I'm alive, don't go for wage work, son. Maybe after I die," she used to say. But this time, Sooranna stood firm. He needed money. "To go to college, it'll cost a lot. There'll be expenses—you don't understand, grandma. Ask uncle if you want," he said.

Aademma didn't know what college was or what kind of studies it involved. But she knew one thing—he must go. He'd studied this far; he should live a better life. Otherwise, he'd end up like her son, working as a laborer for the landlords and dying under their feet. Still, she pleaded. "I'll bring the money somehow. I'll touch someone's feet if I have to. I'll borrow money on interest. But you don't have to do coolie work."

But Sooranna didn't listen. "Then I won't study," he said firmly. There was no way that Aademma could refuse him.

***

Venkanna had formed a close bond with the younger boys in the village, though he was older than all of them.

Everyone called him "Venkadu." He often went to other villages for work. Sometimes, he'd take an entire group with him for a month-long job, save up money, and return. The work would be sowing seeds, harvesting, or digging canals in the summer. If needed, he'd make two separate groups—one for men and one for women. Though he wasn't educated, Venkanna was sharp. He never made a mistake when it came to wages or money calculations. Even those who had studied more than him would be amazed at how accurate he was.

When they went for work in other villages, they'd live right on the land they worked. They'd cook their own food and sleep there—sometimes together, sometimes in small groups. Somehow, by the time they returned home, everyone had money in their hands. It had become their shared truth:

if you work hard and deal fairly, you'll earn. More than just money, they came back with knowledge. Those who stayed back at home believed that those who went out for work knew more about the world—maybe because they had seen other places, other ways.

One day, during the holidays, Sooranna went to Venkanna's house. When he heard that Venkanna was preparing to take a group to another village, Sooranna said, "Venkanna, this time, I want to come too. Take me with your group." Venkanna looked at him in surprise.

"You? No, please don't, da. Your grandmother will scold me."

"No," Sooranna said, "I already asked her. She agreed."

"But still, you can't do physical labor. If something happens, they will blame me." Sooranna tried to convince Venkanna that Venakanna would not be blamed, that he would work hard and, that he needed money for college. Finally, Venkanna stood up and said, "Then let's go ask your grandmother right now."

"Come and ask her right now." Sooranna was afraid they would leave without him. Venkanna asked Aademma what he should do.

"I've begged him so much, Venkanna, but he won't listen. He wants to study … and I want that too. What can I do? I told him to go," she replied. "Be careful, Venkanna. Think of him as your own brother." She had never sent Sooranna outside the village before, and for those four days, her heart stayed with him. She didn't even touch food—not even porridge. She insisted she'd only eat when he came back.

"There is nothing to fear, aunt. I will be with him, right?" said Venkanna. In their homes, everyone was something to someone. Relationships didn't need names; they just existed. They grew up inside those bonds, held together by affection.

That didn't mean there weren't fights, misunderstandings, or moments of anger. Those things did happen. Wrath, jealousy, even revenge—but they never tore the bonds apart. These disputes were always stirred up by landlords and the dramas they created.

***

Venkanna didn't know how to keep track of time using dates. He relied on the moon for that—calculating time by the new and full moon. His calendar was the moon growing and shrinking in size. Any work they started would be after the new moon. If they needed to work between the new moon and the full moon, Venkanna would feel a bit uneasy, but he never made mistakes with his calculations. Funnily, the next day happened to be a full moon. He told Sooranna, "We'll leave the day after tomorrow for work. We'll start early in the morning," and left his house.

The work was clearing mud from the drainage system. The mud had built up in the canal, preventing the water from flowing, and water hyacinth had spread. They also had to raise the height of the edges of the drainage canal.

This kind of work was called *Banta*.[13] Sooranna had heard the name, but he had never done it before.

Since it was summer, they would stop working before the temperature rose too high. They would pick up again in the evening.

The contractor explained everything to Venkanna—how much to dig, how deep, and how wide. Payment was based on the number of *guntas* completed. They measured the breadth, depth, and width of the work, and once a *gunta* was finished, they would mark it with a stick. The wages were based on the number of sticks counted and hours worked. If they finished the said work early, a new job would be given. The more *guntas* they completed, the more they earned. Sooranna soon learned that it wasn't about working long hours—it was about getting the job done quickly and efficiently.

They began working before sunrise. When the heat increased, they would stop.

They saved a little rice and ate it as porridge in the morning. After stopping for a break, they would cook and rest. Some workers would sleep, but Sooranna never did. He would pull out a book and read, as Venkanna noted.

At first, Sooranna found the work difficult. He wasn't allowed to do work that involved use of the hoe or pick. His task was to carry the mud away. He was assigned the job of filling baskets with dirt, then helping others carry the baskets. Sometimes, they worked near a school, and other times, they worked in the fields.

They sang songs while working—one for digging, another for carrying the baskets, and a different one for walking with the load.

Sometimes, there was teasing and laughter at the work site. Other times, everyone was silent, working quickly and without a word. All that could be heard was the sound of footsteps. For Venkanna, dates and time were measured differently. Sooranna's calculations were different, yet somehow both of their internal clocks matched. Venkanna relied on the sun and the moon to tell the time. Sooranna, with no watch, couldn't figure out the time.

In the first week, the supervisor came to check the work and paid them based on the amount completed. Venkanna only knew one thing: a specific amount was paid for each *gunta*.[14] He calculated everything with his hands and feet. He measured the area with his own steps—both length and breadth. His supervisor had never betrayed him.

***

[13]*Banta*—a group of contract laborers working in other villages, staying there until the work is finished.

[14]*Gunta*—a unit of land measurement, equivalent to 1/40 of an acre.

Venkanna asked Sooranna to write down how much they earned as their first day's wage. They took a small amount for daily expenses and left the rest with the supervisor to collect when they returned home. Pointing to Sooranna, Venkanna said, "This boy finished school and is going to college. He joined us during his break." The supervisor smiled, pleased that the boy who was studying was being respected by the workers.

The moon was still a crescent, moving like a swing. Sometimes, there was no line between the sky and the Godavari—their blues merged into one. On full moon nights, the clouds sailed across the sky like boats. Their reflections moved with the river. The boats, the clouds, the moon—they never seemed to sleep. Boats drifted along the Godavari. Just as the fish hid the moon in the water, so too did the clouds hide it in the sky. When the clouds blocked the moon, movements of the night ceased, and time itself paused.

Sooranna was lying on dried grass, staring up at the moon, when Venkanna's voice startled him. "Sooranna, will you drink toddy?" He refused.

They only drank toddy once a week during Banta work. If they drank every day, all the money would be gone.

The workers each brought a small pot and drank together. "We'll keep Sooranna's share for him," someone said, and everyone agreed.

They spent the night of the full moon with games and songs. Sometimes, they even worked at night. Another work group was stationed nearby. They would visit each other now and then—sometimes sharing food, sometimes just talking. Curries, porridge, stories, pain, joy—they shared it all.

As the work neared completion, Sooranna felt the trip had been worth it. He had earned enough to join college and was relieved that his grandmother wouldn't have to worry. Venkanna never let him do the heavier tasks; the whole group gave him the easier work. In return, Sooranna shared what he knew—while eating, before sleeping. They listened with genuine interest. Most of the group had studied only up to fourth or fifth grade before having to drop out for work. That's why they were so drawn to anything related to learning. As they listened to Sooranna, they were often amazed. Is this really our Sooranna? They wondered. They were proud and a little in awe of his intelligence.

***

They thought they would finish the work in two days. And so, they felt like going to see a play being staged in a nearby village. They ate quickly and got ready. Venkanna had seen many dramas before, since he traveled to different villages for work. But for Sooranna, it was the first time.

Just like in their village, there was a temple with a wide open space. A big stage was set up, with colorful curtains hanging in front. Petromax lights were placed along the edges of the stage.

Everyone sat on the ground. Some people brought dry grass to sit on, others brought sacks, and one or two even had small stools. A lot of little kids came and sat right in front of the stage. Some of them were already falling asleep on the ground—how could they even watch a drama like that?

A large crowd had gathered to see the show. Some were whistling. If one person did something, the rest followed—someone would start, and that was enough for the whole crowd to join in. Once something starts, it's hard to stop it. Sooranna's group sat together. Four or five people came over to greet Venkanna. They too had come from other villages for Banta work.

Everyone was talking about the drama, but no one really knew the story. It was a new play for that village. The women sat along the edges of the houses, and the rest of the audience spread out across the open space.

All at once, the bell rang. Sooranna wanted to go closer to the stage to watch the drama, but he waited. It was a new village—what if someone said something?

Someone said, "It's Harishchandra's story."

"No, it's Lava Kusha," said another.

"Eh, it's neither. It's Kurukshetram," someone else chimed in.

"Get lost; it's a regular play, just like our lives," another added.

"If it's Harishchandra, the performers will sing really well!" said a boy. "I watched it the day before yesterday."

While people were still guessing and talking, the harmonium began playing. Suddenly, ten voices joined together in the chorus, singing "Parabrahma."

"Ah, they are starting," said Venkanna. The moment the music started, the kids who were sleeping woke up. After the song ended, a person came out from behind the curtain and greeted everyone. As soon as the curtain moved, the crowd began whistling and cheering.

The man who stepped forward began to speak. He explained why they were performing the play, how long it took to prepare, how they were still working hard, why they were facing difficulties in performing this play, and why they needed the audience's support. Then he stepped back behind the curtain. The moment he stopped talking, the whistling resumed.

The play began.

A boy and his mother were working in a paddy field. The mother tried to convince her son to go work at the landlord's house. "How will we survive if you don't?" she pleaded. But the boy, stubborn, said, "I won't work as a bonded laborer. I want to go to school." That's when the father entered and beat the boy for refusing to work. The boy cried. The women sitting at the edge of the houses sighed and said, "So many hardships, poor boy."

Just then, the landlord appeared on stage.

"You son of a bitch! Look how late it is!" he shouted. "Why haven't you come yet? Who will clean the cow dung? Your mother? Or her husband?"

He began beating the boy and kicked the mother when she tried to stop him. Even when she said, "I will send him, sir," he didn't listen.

He kicked the father.

"Do you think your father is going to clean the shit?"

Will the landlord keep kicking until they reach the house?

Will the boy stop being a bonded laborer?

Will he go to school?

If yes, how will he manage?

What will happen next?

All these questions, more than the whistles, made a loud noise in Sooranna's head.

Whenever the boy tried to run—this way or that—his father caught him, and the landlord would kick him back down.

By the time this had happened a couple of times, the police came in—whistles blaring. Four policemen pushed through the crowd and stormed the stage, beating the actors.

The crowd froze in shock. Children ran in all directions, frightened.

The policemen weren't stopping. They beat those onstage and even those behind the curtain. One constable smashed a petromax light, and as it shattered, he fell into the crowd, hitting anyone he could get his hands on. "Run away, you sons of bitches! You want a drama?" he shouted. The actors on stage didn't flee. They stood still, taking the blows. Behind the curtain, some crew members huddled around the harmonium master, shielding him and the instrument from damage. Another constable leapt from the stage and into the crowd. The moment Venkanna saw this, he yelled, "Run!" and took his companions to the side.

When he reached out to grab Sooranna's hand, Sooranna wanted to ask, "*Why are they beating everyone?*"

Venkanna warned, "No! They'll beat you too. You don't know how these policemen are." He pulled Sooranna aside quickly.

People scattered into the nearby fields, running wherever they could.

No one stopped to ask *why* the police were beating them.

No one dared.

No one knew what happened to the actors, the stage, the lights, or the instruments. There was no one left who could even stop to think.

***

The whole night, Sooranna's mind didn't rest. He kept turning over what had happened. Was there something in that play that angered the police? he wondered. If so, why didn't they just ask them to stop? Why beat everyone? Each question only led to more questions. One sprouted another, and then another—like a tree growing branches in all directions. That's how it was with Sooranna. Once his mind locked onto something, it didn't let go until he found the root of it.

Venkanna asked Sooranna, "Have you ever seen this play?"

"No," he answered. "It would be nice if we could get the text of the play. Then, we would know what happens." Sooranna said, "If the police got angry, then it definitely has to be something amazing."

The whole night Sooranna's head was full of questions, which had no answers.

In the morning, when they all returned to work, the drama was still the main topic. A little while later, the supervisor arrived. Sooranna thought, Maybe he'll know something ... maybe he'll tell us what actually happened.

The supervisor asked, "Did you guys go for the drama last night?" Sooranna was happy upon hearing his question. "Yes, boss," Sooranna replied quickly, "They didn't let the play continue. The police came and beat up the performers. We don't know why."

"That drama is *for* people like you, and that's why the landlords don't like it. They are opposing it. Wherever this drama is being performed, the situation is the same as last night's. Initially, nobody cared about it, as far as I could see. But, what happened in one village is ..." by then the rest of the workers had gathered around to listen.

"One bonded laborer who watched the drama ended up running away from the landlord without saying a word—not even to his family. No one knows how he managed it or who helped him. He disappeared and later joined a school far away. When this happened, the landlords realized it was dangerous to let them continue performing the drama. Nothing had happened to the performers yet, but if the police got involved, their whole operation could be shut down. When the drama reaches its peak, we never know where trouble starts from—suddenly, men show up and begin beating people from all directions. Because of that, the performances were paused for a while. You don't know about policemen. If someone does something the landlords don't approve of, it is the police who do what the landlords want done. That's because the landlords pay them off. It's the same in this case—if laborers watch the drama and decide to stop working, then it becomes difficult to find bonded laborers. So, the landlords stir up the police. And the police don't need a reason. Once they show up, who's going to question them? You saw what happened last night. If this starts happening in one or two villages, no one will dare to act in or even watch the drama. This is what is happening," the supervisor said, hardly pausing for breath. Somewhere deep down, Sooranna felt like the supervisor actually wanted the drama to continue.

"Do you know the people who perform it?" Sooranna asked, wanting to meet them.

"We do not know them. The harmonium player is from our village—he knows where they are. But I don't think the whole group is from one place. They come from different areas, perform the play, and then move on," the supervisor replied.

"Will you show us the harmonium player?" Sooranna requested.

"When are you going back to your village?" the supervisor asked in return.

"Today itself. As soon as you give us the money, we'll leave," said Venkanna.

"Then do one thing," the supervisor said. "After receiving the money, come with me. I'll show you the harmonium master. From there, you can head to your village." Somehow, the supervisor had grown to admire Sooranna. While he worked, there was a depth to him, as if his thoughts were always elsewhere—like he lived in another world. At first, the supervisor assumed it was just because Sooranna was new and still adjusting. But as days passed and Sooranna remained the same—quiet, introspective—he began to feel there was something different about him. He had wanted to talk to him properly for a while, but the chance never came.

By the time all the calculations were done, it was already afternoon. "This time, the work got done without any fights," said Venkanna.

"Right!" someone from the group replied. "Would Sooranna have kept quiet if the calculations had been wrong? Back then, it was only you—people had certain thoughts about you. But even you turned out to be sharp, Venkanna."

"Everything gets better with practice," said Venkanna.

"By the time you are all awake, I will be gone. The harmonium master's village is right next to ours. You know ours, don't you, Venkanna? Last time you came to our place—it's just after that. You just have to cross a small forest. If you ask anyone about the 'harmonium master', they'll guide you." Saying that, the supervisor turned and walked away.

Venkanna distributed the money to everyone. We've saved more this time, everyone thought. They finished the food they had cooked and packed the cooking utensils into a single bag. Then they parted ways—Venkanna and Sooranna took one path, while the rest of the group headed toward their homes.

***

Venkanna and Sooranna crossed the supervisor's village.

Along the way, they stopped a young boy and asked, "Where is the harmonium master's house?"

The boy looked at them with surprise and said, "I don't know." The harmonium master had warned village boys before: *If a stranger asks suspiciously about my whereabouts, don't answer. Tell them only after getting to know them well.* A little further down the path, they came across an old man.

"It is next to the tamarind tree," he answered. Relieved that they had the house address, they thanked him and hurried ahead.

When they reached the house, they stood silently in front of it, unsure how to call out or approach.

From inside, the master spotted them standing quietly.

"Which village are you from?" he asked.

"It is quite far, sir. Mulapally," answered Venkanna. As he spoke, the harmonium master's eyes settled on Sooranna.

"Why did you come?" he asked, stepping out and laying a mat made of toddy leaves on the ground and asking them to sit.

The moment they sat down, he brought them water to drink.

"Tell me, why did you come?"

"We saw your performance last night."

"The beatings were not just for the people who acted but also for those who watched," said the master.

"We also got hit twice," said Venkanna.

"Will the play be available, sir? I want to read it," said Sooranna.

The master looked at the boy, surprised. He wondered what he had found so interesting in the drama that made him want to read it.

"Have you performed in any drama before?" the master asked.

"Small, small scenes," Sooranna replied.

"What? Will you perform this play?" the master questioned.

"We couldn't watch the performance properly, so I want to read the play. I'll return the book after reading," Sooranna said.

"It's not that … I only have one book. It's not printed. It's handwritten," the master explained.

"So this book is not available anywhere else?"

"It is not available. I wrote it myself, word for word, during rehearsals," said the master.

"How did the performers get the thought to stage the play?" Sooranna asked. The master felt this boy had a lot of interest.

"They found the book near the river. They picked it up and took it with them to perform," the master explained.

Sooranna, almost as if begging, said, "I will copy the book and return it to you."

"What are you studying?" asked the master.

"I finished SLC. I've written the exams—we're waiting for the results," answered Sooranna.

"What will you do if you pass?" the master asked.

"He will go to college, sir," Venkanna replied. "He came with us to Banta to be able to join college. As they didn't have enough money, he had to come to work. His grandmother works as a daily wage laborer and brings in what she can." The master felt happy hearing this. Such a focused boy, he thought. He asked again, "What is the name of your village?"

They told him. "Then do one thing," the master said. "Once you get your results, go to Rajavaram. There's a government hostel for college students—meant for Panchama students. There are separate hostels for others, but those charge monthly fees. In this one, you don't have to pay. You'll have no issues with food or accommodation. You just have to concentrate and study. I've enrolled my son there. He finished his first year of Intermediate. When college reopens, he'll go back. It's a good place. If you join, my son will be there—his name is Bheema Rao. He'll help you. Many students are going there. If you find more boys from your village, go and study together. This play also talks about education."

Sooranna's desire to study grew even stronger.

"Then why are policemen beating people? Why are they not letting the performance continue?" questioned Sooranna.

"I told you already," said the master. "This play is about Panchamas leaving bonded labor and choosing to study. The landlords don't like it. In many villages, their laborers are running away and going to school. Wherever the act is performed, if laborers watch it, they stop going to the landlord's house for work. The landlords are scared there won't be any workers left. Since they can't stop it directly, they provoke the police into taking action."

"Can't we stop this? What if we tell the collector?" asked Sooranna.

"We told them—actually, we've told them many times. After a complaint, they stop for a few days. But in different places, the police side with the landlords, depending on their power, and punish us. We have to keep informing them—there's no other way. This is a war. We try to perform, and thcy try to stop it. Let's see how long this goes on," said the master, speaking like an actor from the play.

"If you want to watch the performance, we will be performing in Munivaram in ten days. There will be a big meeting that day. A lot of people will attend. In that place, the police won't be able to interfere," said the master.

"Can I look at the book?" Sooranna asked hesitantly.

"No need, let's go," said Venkanna, speaking like he was afraid some trouble might come from it.

"One minute, Venkanna. Even if I don't read it, I want to touch it at least," said Sooranna.

The master went inside and brought the book. Sooranna felt overjoyed. He stood taller, like he had been given a weapon to fight in a war.

The book was old, with many torn and worn-out pages. It looked like it could fall apart at any moment. Venkanna watched Sooranna closely. Sooranna forgot he was only holding it and read one line out loud.

"You touched it, right? Let's go—it'll be dark by the time we reach home," said Venkanna. Sooranna was like a child who didn't want to let go of his mother's hand. He gave the book back carefully. "We will go now, sir. We will come to watch the performance in Munivaram," both of them said, and turned toward their village.

***

Venkanna was riding the bicycle, with Sooranna on its back. Four others were following behind on their own bicycles. As they neared Munivaram, they began to hear some sounds.

"They might have started," said one person.

"No, someone is talking," said Sooranna.

The wind was carrying the words. The sounds felt scattered—like letters breaking apart, flying in the air, and reaching their ears.

Sooranna focused his mind, trying to catch the words. At times, he could hear them clearly. Someone was speaking in a loud, strong voice. There was anger in the voice—a kind of word war with someone. Ever since he had read the lines from the script, words felt like weapons to him. He felt as if the voice was calling out to everyone: bonded laborers, wage laborers, and landlords—pulling them all into the conversation. He couldn't ask Venkanna to ride faster, but inside, he felt a strong urge to reach quickly and hear more. Just then, there was a loud, "*Dham*!" Everything went dark. Venkanna felt it was probably a flat tire and stopped. The bicycles behind them also came to a halt. Two people got down. Sooranna felt disappointed. He thought they might miss the words being spoken.

"Just a little ahead, there's a bicycle repair shop. Let's walk there," said Venkanna.

They started walking, pushing the three bicycles along with them. Sooranna's mind stayed fixed on the fading voice. He was struggling to keep up with the speed of the words carried by the wind.

"Did you see, Venkanna? Venkatrao gave us a bad bicycle," said one person.

"We will pay him less," replied Venkanna.

They reached the repair shop and showed the bicycle to the mechanic.

The boy at the bicycle shop started repairing the puncture. Maybe because they were all thirsty, the six of them had soda while they waited. The whole time they stood there, Sooranna kept listening to the words carried by the wind.

The bicycle puncture and your wind speed came at the right time, he thought.

Once the repair was done, they started riding toward Munivaram again. This time, they went a bit faster.

***

The stage was set up right next to Munivaram's market road. Guided by the sound from the microphone, they reached the spot where the drama was being performed. By then, a large crowd had already gathered. They tried to move forward, but the people were packed tightly—there was no space to get through. Many people were seated on the stage itself. By the time Sooranna and the others arrived, someone sitting on the stage was speaking: "We must stay united—together, we can achieve anything. These landlords can't do anything to us. Don't be afraid. If injustice happens, rebel against it." With that, he ended his speech.

The crowd burst into claps and whistles.

The curtain fell. It looked like the drama was about to begin, and Sooranna's group started moving closer to the stage.

"They might beat people here too," said Venkanna.

"They might not—there are so many people here," said Sooranna.

A man moved the curtain aside slightly and stepped to the middle of the stage. He began speaking. Sooranna felt like he had seen him somewhere before. He nudged Venkanna and asked quietly, "That's the harmonium master, right?"

"Yes, that is him," replied Venkanna.

Seeing him, Sooranna felt a surge of courage. The man announced that the drama was about to begin and gave a short introduction to what the play would be about.

Sooranna felt like he already knew it.

The curtain fell again. The harmonium started playing. At one point, ten people began singing together.

"It is starting, rey," someone from the crowd said. And it had begun.

Sooranna watched the performance as if he had left his own body. All the situations were just like in his village—the landlords, the bonded laborers. Everyone felt like Viswanatham. The only new things were the different kinds of fights, betrayals, and words. The people on stage reminded him of the people from his village. Only the betrayals were new to him—ones he hadn't known about before. When the laborers in the play formed a committee and fought against injustice, it felt exactly like they were speaking about his own village. The people standing around him felt like the very actors on stage. For a moment, he didn't feel like he was in the real world. He saw a different kind of war—one that hadn't yet happened.

In the play, the laborers saw the scene in which the landlord was getting beaten up by the laborer in the middle of the road. The landlord was beaten up badly and thrown to the road. When that scene happened, some in the crowd were furious. Others clapped, whistled, shouted, and laughed—completely taken by the moment. In the middle of the performance, one person from the crowd tried to run up and hit the actor playing the landlord. People held him back and stopped him. The audience was full of anger. They didn't feel like they were watching a drama anymore—they felt like they were living it.

The play went smoothly. With songs, poems, and music, the crowd became wild with emotion.

They could not meet the harmonium master after the play.

On the way back, Sooranna could think of nothing but the drama. The actors, the incidents—they kept coming back to him. He stayed quiet, not speaking to anyone. Venkanna bought some bananas and gave two to each person. That was their dinner for the night. Sooranna didn't feel hungry. He just held the bananas in his hands.

"We should ask them to perform in our village," said Venkanna.

"No matter how much it costs, we should bring them," said another person.

"Yes, we should," agreed Sooranna.

As they rode back, Sooranna started thinking about writing a script similar to the one they had seen. By then, he had already imagined some actors, incidents, and dialogues. A lot of characters had already emerged from his heart.

He felt like everyone was calling out to him—"Write about us." For the first time, Sooranna felt like he had many friends. He felt there were people to support and encourage him. To stand up to people like Viswanatham, or even the police, he felt like he had the strength of ten elephants. Venkanna kept riding the bicycle without taking a wrong turn, even in such darkness. Maybe he was used to riding at night. Or maybe, he just didn't want to let Sooranna fall.

Everything is probably the same. Habit, perseverance, and being careful are useful in life for anything—otherwise, we fall down, thought Sooranna.

Earlier, they had felt like the bicycle puncture might stop them from watching the drama. But nothing significant happened—they had just arrived a little late. Anything might be delayed, but if we truly want to do something, we will definitely do it, he thought.

Seeing a single bright star in the sky, Venkanna stopped the bicycle near a shop and said, "It's almost morning."

माँ से किसी ने शिकायत की कि बच्चे उपन्यास पढ़ते हैं और पढ़ाई की ओर ध्यान
में था और हमारी उपजाति का था। पुलिस में होना भी उस वक्त बड़ी बात
दोनों परिवारों में कुछ लेन-देन के मामले में मतभेद हुआ और यह रिश्ता टूट

BABURAO RAMJI BAGUL

Dalit Literature Is Not the Literature of Revenge Seekers

A MARATHI ESSAY
TRANSLATED BY MAYA PANDIT

Translator's Note

Baburao Ramji Bagul (1930–2008) may be described as the foremost radical writer in the tradition of modern Dalit literature in Marathi. A poet of intense sociocultural awareness, with a vision for the cultural-political transformation of the classist and caste-ridden society into a just and fair world, he symbolized the dream of Dr. Ambedkar of a modern India with liberty, fraternity, and equality for all. Bagul's sense of Dalit assertion was defined by a wider sense of social, economic, and cultural justice and equality, which he inherited from the Marxist worldview. His literary and cultural-political perspective has the human being at its center in all aspects of the term. As an essayist, inspiring public speaker, organizer of various institutions, creative short story writer and novelist, and poet of rare sensibility, he carved for himself a niche not just in modern Dalit Literature but also in modern Marathi literature. Deeply acquainted with the tradition of the Saint poetry in Marathi, he was also an organic part of the radical Little Magazine movement in the same language, associated with several Little Magazines such as Amhi, Sugawa, Jatak, Dalit Kranti, Dawandi, Magowa, Ranangan, Astitwa, Prameya, *and* Samaj. *His concerns about forging a new language for the articulations of the suppressed voices and their hitherto unexplored areas of experience were at the center of his deep sense of commitment to this movement and his subsequent creative endeavors. He was the Founder President of the Dalit Sahitya Sansad (Parliament of Dalit Literature) in the late seventies and, later, President of the first Vidrohi Sahitya Sammelana (Radical Literary Convention) in Dharavi, the famous slum area where most of the Dalit as well as working-class populations lived in Mumbai in 1999. He also groomed many young writers under his guidance and patronage and helped establish a strong movement of Dalit writers and progressive literature. A major theorist of the Dalit movement, Baburao Bagul has a unique place in the progressive and Dalit movements.*

It is difficult to bring out the radical conglomerations of the syntactic, semantic, and ideological thought structures of Bagul's writing in the span of a few paragraphs. His sensibility was constructed by diverse sociopolitical and cultural forces. As he himself states in the introduction to his poetry collection Vedaadhi Tu Hotas (You Were There Even before the Vedas), *"I have been a follower of Phule and Ambedkar's ideology and I also agree with Darwin, Hegel and Karl Marx's ideas. That is why I advocate the cause of Man, and the greatness of Man"!*[1]

Bagul's radical articulations directly confronted the established protocols of the dominant tradition of Marathi literature. This dominant tradition was marked by a strong belief in a set of supposedly universal human values, narrow proclivities of "upper-caste" concerns and their allegiance to the Brahmanical and so-called pure language, and almost total blindness to, and ignorance of, the material realities of the lives of people on the margins of cities and villages as well as on the margins of social imaginaries. The struggles of Dalits under the leadership of Dr. Babasaheb Ambedkar and of workers under the leadership of Comrade S. A. Dangle, and the resultant clash of values in their struggles, had no place in the corridors of power of the Marathi literary establishment. The frustration of young writers from the middle and working classes and of Dalit writers burst forth with a new vigor and challenge in the form of movements of Little Magazine and Dalit Literature which had hitherto been unknown in Marathi literary culture. Baburao Bagul was a writer at the forefront of both the movements, along with many radical, communist, and progressive writers such as Satish Kalsekar, Daya Pawar, M. N. Wankhede, Namdev Dhasal, Arjun Dangle, and others.

Bagul's collection of poems entitled Vedaadhi Tu Hotas (You Were There Even before the Vedas) *celebrates Man, Human Being, as the foremost material force that has built and shaped the world and rejects God and religion as the creators of the world. Man was there with his strong, creative hands before any God or any religious scriptures. Look at the following lines from the title poem "Vedaadhi tu Hotas":*

It was you who celebrated
The birth of all gods
And the naming ceremonies
Of all the Prophets,

[1]Bagul uses "Man" in contradistinction to "God." The gender-neutral and inclusive expression "human beings" came to be used much later. We have kept close to the original and used the term "Man" because Bagul is concerned with the force and power presented by Man and wants to say that it was not God who created the world as we know it but rather Man who was the real creator of the world. He wants to establish human agency, including both man and woman. That is why he does not make any gender distinction here.

O Man
You named a star as Sun
And the star became the Sun
That is exactly how
The moon became the Moon
You who named all the things in Nature
They came to be known by those names.
Everyone agreed
With all of the things you did
You had the Imagination!
You are the whole and soul of this world.
You are the center of this world
This earth has come alive and become beautiful
Essentially because of you.

All the poems in this collection celebrate Man, and not God, as the creator of the universe. In his poems "He Manasa" ("Invocation to Man"), "Tumche Hat" ("Your Hands"), "Manus" ("Man"), "Pradnyawant Pralaykari Hat" ("The Intelligent and Destructive Hands"), he celebrates the power of the human being. His dream of a just world, another theme of his poems, is articulated in the poem "Jeethey Ghulam Asnaar Nahi" ("There Won't Be a Slave"). His belief is that Man can make earth so beautiful that even God would want to come and become a scavenger here. These poems are very different from the "normal" concerns in the dominant poetic articulations. Bagul's second collection of poetry, Maran Swasta Hot Ahe (Death Is Becoming Cheap), *also illustrates his anguish about the conditions of the oppressed Dalits in society. The angst of the poet bursts forth in the following words:*

The man who erred by taking birth in this land
Must correct himself now …
By leaving this land … or … by waging terrible wars.

"Woman" also forms a major concern in his poetic and literary universe. In fact, women, especially the oppressed Dalit women, form a major theme of many of his literary creations. His story "Mother" ("Aai"), one of the best among the modern Indian short stories, portrays the shattering dilemma in a widow's life and exposes the sham culture of valorization of Motherhood in Indian society. The story exposes the multilayered contradictions in the life of a widowed woman who works as a construction worker. The compulsions and demands of working under a contractor, the desires of her own body, and her child's expectations from his mother (the seeds of which are sown in school education with the literature that celebrates motherhood) violently clash to destroy the emotional stability and equilibrium of the lives of both the child and the mother and alienate the child from the mother. His

novel Suud (Revenge) *portrays the plight of a woman undergoing sexual oppression and shows how she found a release in the company of a spiritual man who helped her carve a way of salvation for herself.*

Bagul's short stories shock the reader into an awareness of the horrifying conditions of life to which the worker, the laborer, and the ordinary wage earner are subjected. The stories in his collection Jevha Me Jat Chorli Hoti (When I Concealed My Caste) *portray human beings reduced to a state of beasts of burden and at the mercy of the dominant forces of oppression. His characters, like live wires, expose the bleak and dark world of sufferings of various kinds. And yet they all retain the essentially humane vision of life.*

Baburao Bagul's essays and speeches contain his extraordinary commitment to the values of liberty, fraternity, and equality. He is an internationalist in all senses of the term. His famous Presidential Address at the Literary Convention in Mahad, organized by the Maharashtra Bouddha Sahitya Sabha (i.e., the Buddhist Literary Organization of Maharashtra), in 1971, and other addresses at different programs organized by the progressive and Dalit writers' organizations, opened up a map of wide horizons of new intellectual, aesthetic, and political-cultural values that he defined from his location in the Dalit literary movement. Especially important are essays like "Dalit Sahitya He Tar Mansanche Sahitya" ("Dalit Literature Is Essentially the Literature of Human Beings"), "Hindu Sahitya wa Jatiwad" ("Hindu Literature and Casteism"), "Dalit Sahityachi Disha" ("The Direction of Dalit Literature"), "Dalit Sahitya Suudwadyanche Sahitya Nahi" ("Dalit Literature Is Not the Literature of Revenge Seekers"), and "Dalit Hach Yuganayak" ("The Dalit Is the Protagonist of the Epoch"). These essays exemplify his wide concerns, ranging from a critical examination of the tradition of the dominant literature of the "upper castes" to the delineation of his expectations for the Dalit creative articulations, which had been banished for ages from the precincts of the dominant literary concerns. In answer to the question, "What is the origin of the suffering in the society?" he replies in his essay "Dalit Sahitya He Tar Mansanche Sahitya" ("Dalit Literature Is Essentially the Literature of Human Beings") in the following words:

> When society witnessed the sense of property and ownership, many exploitative systems came into being, such as religious systems that popularized rites and rituals and spread ideas of heaven and hell and principles that sanctioned exploitation. Many new concepts began to be circulated as per the requirements of the exploitative power structures.

Bagul subjected the cultural politics of the dominant "upper castes," especially the Brahmanical systems, to an objective critique and continued in the provocative tradition of Mahatma Phule, Shahu Maharaj, and Dr. Ambedkar of debunking the myth of the superiority of the upper castes. Thus, he brought a new critical perspective into the Dalit Literary Movement.

Another important point that Bagul emphasized concerned the meaning of the term Dalit. In his essay "Dalit Mhanje He Jug wa Jeevan Navyane Mandanara" ("Dalit Is the One Who Redefines This World and Life"), he said:

> Many take umbrage to the term "Dalit." They are scared by our definitions of Dalit. That is why in order to cause a rift amongst us, they deliberately associate many wrong meanings with this term. But brothers, we have declared that the term Dalit signifies the force that will destroy the Varna system and all its intellectual rigmarole. We have declared that Dalit is the force that will transform this world and define life from a new perspective. Dalit is the one whose hands have been charged by this epoch with a new intellectual vigor, and empowered with the strength of the new weapons and new sciences. Our definition of the term Dalit incudes all the oppressed in the world: the Blacks, Whites and Red in the Americas and the Black, White and Yellow from the Asian countries.

He appealed to people to take forward the Cultural Revolution of Dr. Ambedkar to all the oppressed sections everywhere. He also proclaimed that ultimately the philosophy of materialism, atheism, and democratic socialism would overcome the dominance of the Varna system and the inequality it has generated.

Bagul was often criticized for his so-called closeness to the left ideology by some Dalit writers, but he never compromised on the issue of uniting all the oppressed. In fact, the Dalit Panthers, the militant organization of radical young Dalit men, was vertically divided on the issue of closeness to the Left ideology. Bagul was an inspiration to the formation of the Dalit Panthers, but later on two groups developed within the Dalit Panthers; one was led by Arjun Dangle, Namdev Dhasal, and their allies, and the second was led by Raja Dhale, along with J. V. Pawar and some other activists. Arjun Dangle and Namdev Dhasal were close to Baburao Bagul and supported a larger unity of all progressive forces, including all the left parties and groups. Raja Dhale and J. V. Pawar, however, thought that unity with the left would be harmful to the Dalit interests. On this issue the Dalit Panther split and gradually lost its political edge. Bagul's position was, in a sense, vindicated.

It is very difficult to discuss all the aspects of the work of this great intellectual, writer, essayist, novelist, poet, and short story writer in the short span of an introduction. His wide and humane perspective and his map of transformative politics through a Dalit movement in collaboration with the forces of left ideology impress us with his vision of a new life. His tremendous creative energy, amazing vitality, and astounding dynamism remain unsurpassed in the history of modern Marathi literature.

Context for the Essay:

This is the text of "Presidential address delivered by Baburao Bagul at Mahad, at the second convention of the Bouddha Sahitya Sabha,[2] on February 13 and 14, 1971," in *Dalit Sahitya: Ek Abhyas*, ed. Arjun Dangle (Mumbai: Maharashtra Rajya Sahitya Sanskruti Mandal, 1978), 204–212.

My brothers and sisters,

This is a grand felicitation program that you have organized for me, and I am really overwhelmed by your affection and love. But I do not feel that I have done any work that deserves such grand felicitation. There are many older writers of repute and also writers who have been quite prolific. Actually, they should have been the recipients of such a great honor. I have written comparatively far less than them. What I write is quite explosive, but it is not "prolific." I have yet to write much more. I want to portray in words the people I have seen in my life. There are so many experiences that I have yet to articulate. There is so much that I have to write about. Yet you have honored me today for my writing. And this is happening at a famous place, Mahad, that is known as the first battlefield of the Dalits fighting for liberation from their oppression. This was the first of its kind of revolt in Indian history. The revolt, that sacred and hallowed event, took place under the leadership of a man who was as great as the Buddha, Dr. Babasaheb Ambedkar. This place, Mahad, is the most sacred place, and it is a great honor to me that you are felicitating me at this particular place. I am very happy and grateful for this great honor and accept the love of all my brethren with great humility.

I have experienced the tremendous love you have for me at several places and times. And I also love you like the great saint Tukaram Maharaj.[3] You are the great heroes of my writing. I have decided to narrate the stories of your life through my writing. That is because nobody had ever sung the stories and spirit of your lives. Nobody had ever sung your songs. Not because you were not heroes but because the people who could sing songs about your heroism were never free to do so. Their voices were throttled. But I am free, and I have not allowed my voice to be silenced. That is why I have decided to sing and celebrate your heroism. Both you and I have been born in this

[2]The Bouddha Sahitya Sabha (Buddhist Literary Organization) was an organization of the Dalit intellectuals converted to Buddhism. They would organize seminars, speeches, and discussions on Dalit issues.

[3]Tukaram Maharaj was one of the great Marathi Saints in the Bhakti tradition in the seventeenth century.

prison in this unfortunate, fateful country. Before Babasaheb came, we all were prisoners of the same dark age. We were all suffering the same agonies of hell. But today we have seen the light. However, our untouchability has not gone away. Our suffering has not ended. That is why Dalit Literature also will not end. Dalit Literature considers untouchability and slavery, inequality, and suffering, as its sworn enemies. Dalit Literature is literature which advocates the liberation of all human beings; it considers the Human Being as supreme and opposes and contests the supremacy of certain sections of society on the basis of caste, varna, and race. Some time ago, a friend had abused us by saying that we are racists. But let me ask you firmly and frankly, how can we be called racists? We have literally been burnt in the fire of race and caste superiority. You know the story in the Mahabharata where the forest called Khandav Vana[4] was burnt down by the Panadavas to establish their empire; you know that only a few creatures could save themselves from the fire. We have experienced firsthand the terrible fire of injustice and oppression imposed upon us by the caste and race systems. That is what we oppose. This is not just a recent event; our opposition to, and struggle against, caste and race supremacy has been going on since Dr. Ambedkar began the struggle against them. There are hundreds of struggles that evidence this.

We are not contemptuous toward others. Whatever little literature we have produced so far does not evidence any criticism of any particular caste. We are against the social, psychological, and intellectual system that exists here. Thus, we have undertaken an extremely difficult task. Many reformers and intellectuals could see their enemies in front of them, and in that period it was quite justifiable for them to consider those elements as their enemies. The Marxists and Socialists can identify their enemies in front of them. Many political parties consider their opponents as their enemies. But for us the enemy is invisible. This enemy exists in the religious books, in the language, in the thoughts, and in the mind. Our war is against an enemy which is omnipresent and powerful yet remains invisible.

This war had begun right from the time when British rule was established in India. Many Hindu reformers tried to attack this invisible enemy, but those attacks were comparatively feeble. That was because the Hindu reformers had only a limited goal in their minds. They wanted to reform the Hindu, especially the Hindu middle-class family. They wanted to bring

[4]Khandav Vana: This was the name of a great forest near the river Yamuna. The story is from the epic Mahabharata. The Pandavas wanted to build their empire there, though the forest was under the protection of God Indra. God Agni, the Fire God, had insatiable hunger, and God Krishna and Arjuna went against God Indra. They helped Agni burn the forest to satiate his hunger. Only seven creatures escaped death by burning. Here, Bagul uses the image of the Khandava Vana to highlight the immensity of caste oppression.

a system which would enhance the happiness of this family. But they had to suffer even for this limited goal. Of course, they did face the challenge of reforming the traditional family and took the reform movement ahead. The thought of social restructuring gathered some force, and there was some progress in that direction.

But one must admit with great regret that our social reformers never thought of the entire Indian community and the masses of people in it. In Europe there are so many examples of reformers being burnt to death, hanged, or driven out of the cities as outcasts. However, nothing of the kind happened here. One of the reasons may be that the political power here was not averse to reforms. Had it been the rule of the Hindus or Muslims, then probably the reformers would have had to suffer such punishments. They might have had to sacrifice their lives. And yet, in spite of the fact that the political rule was sympathetic to reforms, none of the reformers proposed any argument for the entire reconstruction of the society and annihilation of the caste and varna system. Why didn't they do so? The major reason for this was their commitment to their own caste. Also, they were scared of being excommunicated. They wanted this system as it exists because this system has given them all that they wanted. How can they, who have got everything, ever propose an idea of an all-encompassing revolt? Even today it would be impossible to find anything which goes even a little closer to the revolutionary thoughts that Dr. Babasaheb Ambedkar proposed and propounded.

There are examples aplenty. Lokamanya Tilak,[5] who is glorified as the creator of the Indian discontent, was quite scared of being excommunicated. Several leaders who were his colleagues were no exception. They felt cowed before this dread of excommunication. This is a special feature of our Indian leadership. That is because our leadership is still limited to only a few upper-caste people, as there is a lack of education and dearth of opportunities for the oppressed classes. The Hindu religion and Hindu culture are especially staunchly against giving opportunities to others and their education. If one looks at the national movement for freedom, one witnesses that when the other castes and communities received education and got opportunities, their own leaders rose up; however, these leaders began fighting against one another. Not one of the leaders among them ever tried to stop this infighting among themselves. They never proposed any plan for the development and progress of all the people. Even the so-called all-encompassing Gandhian thought is no exception to this tendency. When the untouchables began to unite under the leadership of

[5]Lokamanya Tilak: A strong leader of the Indian National Congress in the first two decades of the twentieth century. It is said that he had to suffer punishment for the sin of traveling to England, crossing the seas. He was probably scared of the wrath of the rigidly orthodox Brahmin community.

Dr. Babasaheb Ambedkar, the issue of untouchability began to be raised in the Rashtriya Sabha[6] with increasing intensity. The same has happened in history too. There were many invaders who came into India; they belonged to various religions and communities, but none of the invaders had any desire to make changes in the Indian society. The structure of the Hindu society is so rigid and so tightly woven that the ordinary common man has no value there. He was not even considered as a human being. But the common people, to whichever caste they may belong, do have a right to live. The invaders entered India and occupied the central place in the huge fort carefully built by the society and stayed there in great comfort. They entered India, occupied the throne, and got servants already produced by the system here. Huge money flowed to their throne. The Hindu society is a system which favors the ruling State power and tries hard not to create any trouble for them. The Hindu religion considers the King as a form of God and one who has a divine element of Lord Vishnu. The many principles of the Hindu religion are quite supportive of the feudal system. That is why the political powers who had no experience of the system of untouchability simply allowed it to remain as it was without any interference or attempt to change it. The entire system of exploitation had already been created by the producers of untouchability and kept ready for the rulers to exploit for their own purposes. And which political power would want to reject this readymade system of exploitation?

That is why we say that the Hindu religion is born out of a feudal system, and it will always try to strengthen that system. It nurtures the feudal ideology and the feudal mentality that derives from it. The feudal system had no place for the woman and for the slave. In fact, they had no place in the Hindu religion itself.

No one had even tried to change this situation. The Hindu Saints have always been praised for their great social work. But even they never tried to change the situation of women and the Shudras and Ati-Shudras.[7] On the other hand, they spoke about women with great contempt and ridicule. They

---

[6]The Indian Association (also known as the Indian National Association) was a nationalist organization that aimed to promote the political, intellectual, and material advancement of the people of India. Dr. Ambedkar was not part of this organization. He founded other parallel organizations focused on the upliftment of marginalized communities, such as the Bahishkrit Hitakarini Sabha and the Independent Labour Party. The Indian Association focused on broader political and intellectual advancement of the Indians, while Dr. Ambedkar's organizations addressed the specific issues of social discrimination, inequality, and political representation faced by the Depressed Classes (Dalits). With Dr. Ambedkar's rise on the political horizon, the Indian Association began to discuss the issue of untouchability.

[7]The Hindu hierarchy consists of Brahmans at the top, followed by Kshatriyas (the warrior class), then Vaishyas (the merchant class), and then Shudras (those who performed diverse tasks related to agriculture). The Ati-Shudras were not included in this list; they were thrown out of the system. They were supposed to serve all the other castes above them. They were considered the lowest of the low, the most polluting and despised section of the society.

considered women as the greatest obstacle in the attainment of Moksha.[8] They always spoke about women in such a way as to create a heinous, disgraceful, and obnoxious perception about them in the society. They considered the untouchables as unholy, and none of them ever tried to critically analyze the principles that nurtured and strengthened untouchability in the society. On the contrary, they upheld the unjust system. Their sweet and powerful words intruded this poisonous thought into each house and into each person. They had a great impact on the minds of people. They virtually broke the spirit of the downtrodden people. None of the Saints challenged the theory of rebirth and the karma theory, which advocated the thought that one has to suffer for the sins committed in the last birth, which is why one is born in a lower caste. This is, for them, a divine arrangement. Nobody asked what exactly was meant by the artifice and subterfuge implicit in the concepts of karma, hell, heaven, and "atma" (the soul). They never tried to examine whether the suffering of people was given to them by God or caused by the feudal religious system. Not that the Saints were linked to or bound by the State power. Today you will find many fake Saints who are in the service of the State power. The Saints in the past were not like that. But the system was created so craftily and cunningly by the cruel and draconian architects of our society that our Saints accepted it willingly, blindly, without challenging it. They criticized women and the Shudras in such rude, derogatory, and abusive language that they presented them as the epitome of everything contemptuous, unholy, and disdainful.

Thus, when the Saints accept the rules and conventions of the Manusmriti[9] and the theory of rebirth and Karmawada,[10] they uphold the feudal system and untouchability.

That is why so many Saints were born, and they even rose to fame, along with the gods that they worshipped, but the society remained where it was, without changing a bit. Untouchability did not receive any blow, not even a slight one. The upper-caste Saints, or the intellectuals belonging to the upper castes, never handled the problem of untouchability. Also, the untouchables never rebelled against their oppression even once. Till Babasaheb arrived on the scene, the untouchable communities accepted their slavery without any complaint. They never realized that their slavery was created by those people who controlled the religious, cultural, and political power in society. They would consider it as a divine disciplinary system forced upon them by the divine police officers in heaven. Their ignorance had convinced them that their birth in the untouchable castes was a result of their sins in the previous

[8]Moksha: In the Hindu view, moksha is the ultimate release of the soul from the cycle of being born again and again.

[9]Manusmriti is the ancient book of Hindu laws that advocated the varna and caste system. Dr. Babasaheb Ambedkar undertook a program to burn it publicly.

[10]Karmawada: The theory that your next birth is determined by the deeds you do in the present birth.

life. They endured all oppression without uttering a single word of protest in the hope that the merit thus earned in this life by their mute suffering of every injustice would give them a better life in the next birth; that is, they would be born in a higher caste.

The creators of society had deliberately kept the untouchable away from all education, culture, knowledge of weaponry, and any kind of power so that he would not dare to rebel even in the slightest manner. If man is compelled to live in such conditions, man does not remain *man* anymore. Now man is also a creation of Nature, which is basically dynamic and creative; hence, man also should be dynamic and creative. Man's body and his inner energy constantly strive for creation. Creativity is part of his being human. If the inner energies in man do not receive any opportunity for expression or articulation, they rust away and go to waste. Man gets reduced to being an animal. He gets crushed under the pressure of tremendous lethargy and inertia. I have been visiting many villages and have seen men who are nothing but living corpses. I become furious at this destruction of human abilities, enthusiasm, labor, and intelligence caused by the deliberate and ruthless attitudes and actions of the powers that be. But what is the point of getting furious? Those who had wreaked this violence may have possibly felt quite happy with themselves; they must have lived comfortably on the loot they had collected. They had fed poison to the people and kept them quiet and docile, as a result of which any possible revolt against them was completely suppressed and silenced. But their silence and suppression had reduced the oppressed to being like lifeless men. They had no strength left to fight against the foreign invaders, and as a result, the foreign invaders were able to conquer India.

But sometimes the untouchable joined hands with the foreign invaders for the opportunity it gave him to put to use his inner energies, to demonstrate his power, and for the pleasure it gave him to live as a creative man and to enjoy the pleasure of fighting with a weapon in his hand. The people who joined the Muslim armies and increased their power, or those who joined the British armies, were indeed untouchables, though they were not many in number. But the inhuman and savage system here has not stopped their destruction even now. The tremendous power of the tribal people and nomadic tribes is being totally and completely wasted. That power and energy of the tribal people finds expression in their anger and desire for change. I don't think there is any other system in the entire world which has wasted and destroyed so many human beings as in our country.

There is a huge difference between the slave system in India and similar systems in the rest of the world. Except for India, slaves all over the world have rebelled against their oppressors. As Marx says, the history of the world is the history of class struggle all over the world, except in India. It is the Indian leaders who have broken down this rebellion. Those who should have rebelled were so much under the influence of the gods in heaven and the ideology of *karma vipaka*,[11] that one has to suffer for sins of past life in this life, that they never rebelled against this belief. As a result, the people in the lower ranks of the society, especially the untouchables, were completely wasted, and their abilities were allowed to decay.

Indian life had remained in this decayed state until the British came to India. The British brought with them new technology, machinery, and new thoughts. This caused quite a huge turbulence in the society. But the lowermost layers of society remained in the same condition. And even today a great number of people are still very quiet, they have not been able to raise their voices. But once Babasaheb arrived upon the scene, these masses were furiously awakened. Dalit literature was born out of the furnace of Dr. Babasaheb Ambedkar's thoughts and the tremendous turmoil caused by them in society.

But Dalit literature is not the literature of revenge seekers. Dalit literature is also not about spreading hatred in society. Dalit literature firstly champions the greatness of man and his liberation. Besides, Dalit literature is a historical necessity as well. That is why it adopts a separate and different name for itself. A poem written by a Dalit and someone in America will still be poems. Whether they are good or bad can be decided later. But both of them have to be accepted as poems. Just as this is true, so it is true that this literature has to be called Dalit Literature. There are two reasons for this. The first reason is that you have produced it; it is your force that has been behind its creation. And the second reason is that it is also an integral part of the literature in this country, India, so it is very much part of Indian Literature.

Let us first consider your condition at present. You have absorbed the fire of the Ambedkarian struggle; you have internalized that fire and become flames of the struggle. Remember, when the Satyagraha of the Chavdar Tale[12] took place here, in Mahad, Dr. Babasaheb Ambedkar had compared your meeting with the National Council of the French Revolution, and you passed the resolution proclaiming Liberty, Equality, and Fraternity, the three principles of the French Revolution, as the three principles of your struggle too. The French National Council had also passed seventeen resolutions of this kind in 1789.

Dr. Babasaheb Ambedkar had said the following while addressing the huge meeting at that time, "The European historians had applied insulting names to this French Revolution, but I will not do so. That is because this

[11]The same as Karmawada. See footnote no. 10. Karma means "work," and "vipaka" means the result or effect. The assumption is: Good work earns you merit, and bad work earns you sin. So, your next birth depends on your "karma."

[12]Chavdar Tale is a lake in Mahad in Maharashtra. The Chavdar Tale Satyagraha, also known as the Mahad Satyagraha, was a significant event in the Dalit movement. On March 20, 1927, Dr. B. R. Ambedkar led untouchable people to this lake in order to secure the right for untouchables to use water from a public tank. This was a defiant act that signified a powerful assertion of the human rights of Dalits and a rejection of the caste system's discriminatory practices against Dalits who were not allowed to access public water tanks.

revolution ushered in the great fortune of the development of Europe. Our meeting will also open up the floodgates of good fortune for India, our country." He had considered you revolutionaries.

You *are* revolutionaries. You have learnt from Dr. Babasaheb's movement to reject a lot of dead wood. You have gone way beyond the initial rejections from the dominant literary systems. You have rejected many customs, conventions, and concepts like God, dharma, and religion. This power to reject is no less significant. It shows grit and daring and courage. Even great intellectuals have been unable to match themselves to this task.

Even great social reformers have been afraid of the social boycott they would face as a result of their rejecting established norms. Tilak took punishment (for his travel to a foreign land); he agreed to purify himself as per the Brahmanical customs because he was scared of their social boycott. But you managed to just burn off and reduce to ashes the evil conventions that had managed to destroy human beings of flesh and blood. You showed tremendous courage in the beginning of this struggle. The same Manusmriti, before which all governments and all our great Saints who were able to see their own death, had bowed their heads, you dared to burn and create a huge uproar all over the country. It created a great turmoil across India.

You are really great in many senses of the term. You are like the revolutionaries that Marx had described. And you are easily included in the definition proposed by the Buddha.

We are utterly convinced that you have the power to create a new epoch. That is why we call our literature by your name. You are now people who are marching forward. Today, at this moment, everyone should be marching forward to wrench greatness away from the future, which holds it in its hands. But instead we witness many institutions, political parties, and many individuals running toward the historical past. They receive inspiration and life from the heroes in history. They are digging out the old enmities and wars from history. This turning back to history and closing one's eyes to the future does not augur well for the country. It cannot be a sign of being alive. They do not trust the future because in order to do so, they will have to destroy their class pride. But that is precisely what they do not want to do. That is why they desperately turn to the historical past. But you, on the contrary, are marching forward toward the future. You are searching for the new light.

The present lies under your feet. And the future is in front of your eyes. Your history is the history of liberating man. Your ideal is Dr. Babasaheb, that great worshipper of knowledge. Your ideal is the Buddha, who is the ocean of Karuna itself.

The tremendous inspiration and motivational force behind Dalit Literature is located in the terrible humiliation of human beings. The inspiration and light come from there. The system has reduced living men to corpses by creating a deadlock around them. That is why it is the human being that is at the center of Dalit Literature. Dalit literature is the proclamation of man's freedom. It considers man as the supreme being and assigns God and religion a lower place than man. A human being is an epic poem. The emotions of man are like the great seasons. It is man who has created this world and beautified it. It is man's hands that have become the chariots of progress and carried it forward. Revolutions are created by the hands of the laboring man. That is what we believe. That is why we consider this epoch as our own epoch because it has liberated man from his suffering and bondage.

Because we believe that man is at the center of our thought, any perspective that considers man as a criminal, murderer, debauch, sinner, and insignificant being like an insect is nothing but absolutely contemptible for us. We have experienced this deadly contempt all our life. This contempt is nothing but an insult to humanness itself, and it is embedded in, and revered by, the Varna and the caste system. The writers who propound this view of us have come from the same class that had propounded such an ideology of contempt for ages.

This place, Mahad, had witnessed a stupendous and colossal expression of the great fury of man in 1927. But not even one Marathi poet or writer either took note of it or chose to describe it. Yet out of that colossal rage a new light was born. That moment signaled liberation of the oppressed. And yet not even one newspaper noted it. Why, even Shri. Ma. Mate, whom we idolize as "Mahar Mate," also has ignored and therefore devalued that rage. There is not a single novel on this revolutionary and significant event of Mahad. What are the reasons for this colossal neglect? Efforts to seek an answer to this question reveal that the writers of Marathi are Hindus, and that is why they have never even tried to glimpse the reality of the Maharwada and the Mangwada. As Dr. Ketkar has argued, the Marathi writer has always been interested in the life of the Brahman community living in Pune, especially in the Sadashiv Peth area, and has kept on producing literature based on that slice of narrow life.

When the Hindu rightist movements began to grow, this same Hindu upper-caste writer began to write against the Muslims. However, when the Gandhian movement began, there were talks of Hindu-Muslim unity, and a movement for the eradication of untouchability got public acceptance. Then some of the female protagonists or side heroes of a few literary works by some Hindu writers began to come from the untouchable people. But most of these characters were quite fake, and they were basically from the middle class. There were many struggles of the untouchables, such as the Kala Ram Agitation for Temple Entry,[13] but these never formed part of the subjects of literary works.

---

[13]There is a temple of God Ram in Nashik called the Kala Ram. The Dalits were not allowed entry into the temple. Ambedkar organized a large protest outside this temple on March 2, 1930, in order to enter into the temple. Many Dalit protesters arrived in the town by trucks; they surrounded the temple by sitting down on the ground around it.

The basic reason why they don't appear in the Hindu writers' literature is that these writers are scared of undergoing various experiences of an essentially different kind, and besides, they are scared of their readers as well. Even many reformers were scared of being excommunicated; now, are these writers also scared of being excommunicated? Or does their training from early childhood in their families to treat the untouchables with contempt prohibit them from going to the Maharwadas?

We believe this is the true explanation of why they never visited our untouchable localities. The woman in Marathi novels and plays is traditional, sketched by the writers on the model presented by the traditional Shastras and Puranas. Unless they portray women in that way, they probably do not get any artistic satisfaction. Dalit Literature, however, has rejected this training in literary culture. That is why it can portray human beings, their agony and ecstasy, and their desires and emotions in a realistic and compelling manner. Dalit writers will help many excommunicated beings and their emotions, which so far have never been embraced with love and compassion by Marathi writers, to obtain an entry into the province of literature. Marathi will cease to have residents only from the Brahmanical Sadashiv Peth area and will be crowded by many others from diverse regions. The Marathi language will be enriched by many new words and imaginative expressions, and its literature will truly be the literature of many, many people.

TULSIRAM

Death Grounds

AN EXCERPT FROM THE HINDI MEMOIR *MURDAHIYA*
TRANSLATED BY JOEL LEE

Translator's Note

Dr. Tulsiram's Murdahiya *is an extraordinary text. The surprise begins with the title itself. A word not found in dictionaries of standard Hindi but redolent of the regional vernacular,* murdahiya *means neither (Hindu) cremation ground nor (Muslim) cemetery but something of both, and more as well. The death grounds thus evoked by the title then provide the unexpected organizing metaphor for a story of individual and collective* life. *At one level, the book is an autobiography, a chronicle of a scarred and enchanted childhood. At another, it is a kaleidoscopic tour of village life in India in the two decades following the country's independence, a scrupulously observed narrative of everything from irrigation to exorcism, children's rhymes to caste councils, buffalo husbandry to bonded labor, Dalit deities to Brahmin weddings, drought survival tactics to the rise of leftist politics among the peasants of eastern Uttar Pradesh. The detail of an ethnographic compendium is suffused with the insight of a Buddhist coming-of-age story. In its scope, structure, substance, and style,* Murdahiya *is a book that stands apart.*

When Murdahiya *was published in 2010, Dr. Tulsiram—who goes by one name—was known not for his association with rural India but rather, to the contrary, for his expertise on Russia, Iran, and left transnationalism. A professor in the School of International Studies at Jawaharlal Nehru University (JNU) in Delhi, Dr. Tulsiram, then aged sixty, researched and wrote extensively on the history of communism in Iran, Soviet–Iranian relations, the Angolan independence movement, and political developments in post-Soviet states. He spoke Dari and Russian and advised dozens of M.Phil. and Ph.D. students in International Relations. As* Murdahiya *makes clear, though, his early childhood did not in any conventional sense pave the way for such a career. He was born in 1949, two years after India's freedom from British rule, to a family of Dalit field laborers attached by intergenerational servitude—the "ploughman's bond"—to a family of*

Brahmin landlords. No one in his family was literate. Pocked and partially blinded by a severe case of smallpox, Tulsiram was regarded in the village as an evil omen, a vehicle of inauspiciousness. His participation in school was a source of constant tension in his family and the wider community; village Brahmins and his own uncles actively discouraged his studying beyond primary school. Captivated by the story of Gautam Buddha's escape from family life to pursue knowledge, Tulsiram fled his village in 1964. After brief stints in Azamgarh and Calcutta, he came to Varanasi, where he studied at Benares Hindu University. Ten years later he moved to Delhi, where he completed his doctorate at JNU and subsequently joined the faculty. After Murdahiya, *Dr. Tulsiram composed a second part to his autobiography,* Manikarnika, *focused on the period in which he lived in Varanasi. He began work on a third part, dealing with his life in Delhi, but was unable to complete it due to deteriorating health. He died in 2015. According to his daughter, in his adult life Dr. Tulsiram never returned to the village.*

Lively debates over what constitutes Dalit literature—whether particular thematic foci, aesthetic codes, or political commitments should be considered criteria rather than or in addition to the social location of the author—have accompanied the emergence and popularization of this category of writing in India's multiple literary spheres in recent decades. In Hindi, the efflorescence of cultural production presented and discussed as Dalit literature since the 1990s is tightly bound to the genre of autobiography—or rather, ātmakathā, *or self-story. Poetry, short stories, and novels also appear in 1990s and 2000s Hindi Dalit literature, but it is autobiography that has often dominated representation of and critical response to the field. Mohan Das Namishray's* Apne Apne Pinjre *(1995), Omprakash Valmiki's* Joothan *(1997, English translation in 2003), Kausalya Baisantry's* Dohrā Abhishāp *(1999), Shymlal's* Ek Bhangi Kulpati kī Ankahī Kahānī *(2004), and Surajpal Chauhan's* Tiraskrit *(2002) and* Santapt *(2006) are among the defining landmarks of this body of work. To an extent these Hindi works drew inspiration from an earlier wave of Marathi autobiographical writing by Dalits, among them Daya Pawar's* Baluta *(1978), Baby Kamble's* Jina Amucha *(1986), and Vasant Moon's* Vasti *(1998), all subsequently translated into English.*

When Murdahiya *appeared in 2010, then, it contributed to an acknowledged genre—the publisher advertises on the back cover that the book has achieved renown "among Dalit autobiographies [*dalit ātmakathāon mei*]"—and a robust if still young literary tradition. The book shares with its predecessors certain features: an unpretentious style, interest in the social conditions of political awakening, and a narrative focus broadly oriented toward collective rather than individual life.* Murdahiya *in these respects fits Sharmila Rege's characterization of Dalit self-writing as "testimonio," a genre of witness-bearing that violates "the boundaries set by bourgeois* *autobiography" and communicates "the situation of a group's oppression ... and struggle."*[1] *But in other ways* Murdahiya *carves a rather unusual path compared with other Dalit autobiographies. One notable difference is that the exemplary life and writings of Bhimrao Ambedkar, which play a decisive role in the political awakening of the protagonists of many Dalit autobiographies, are largely absent in* Murdahiya. *While Ambedkar becomes important to Tulsiram later in life, in his childhood it is the inspiration of local communist activists and the example of the historical Buddha—not as received through Ambedkarite Buddhist networks but as encountered in a school textbook in tenth standard—that provide the catalyst for his emancipatory trajectory.*

Another distinction is the attention Tulsiram gives to ghosts, goddesses, religious practitioners, and local understandings of unseen force, as well as the ambiguity of the narrative toward this dimension of community life. To be sure, observation of "folk" beliefs and practices is not infrequent in Dalit autobiographies. Rarely, though, does the supernatural so thoroughly pervade the narrative as it does in Murdahiya, *and more rarely still are those engaged in such activity—like Tulsiram's grandmother, a devotee of the Dalit goddess Chamariya Mai—spared judgment by the author on this count. For a number of authors, commitment to emancipatory Dalit politics entails a necessarily radical repudiation of ways of life associated with the old rural caste order, particularly in the domain of belief. Baby Kamble's depiction of the goddess possessions she witnessed among her elders in her childhood as utterly fraudulent, and her summary assessment that "our people rotted and perished by following such a superstitious way of life," are characteristic.*[2] *Tulsiram does not refrain from pointing out the deleterious consequences of certain belief-based stances, such as his uncles' refusal to take his ailing grandmother to a hospital, and he notes with a cool Marxist eye the mechanisms by which particular metaphysical notions popular in the village secure for dominant castes direct material profit. On the whole, though, the ghosts and goddesses that populate* Murdahiya *are shielded from categorical dismissal and granted a certain ambiguity of status. The vividness and palpability of malevolent and auspicious forces enabled by this narrative agnosticism make sensible the terror and wonder of village life. Depicting the supernatural as his family members and others understand it, Tulsiram resists subjecting the people of his village to caricature. Rather, as Shivani Kapoor puts it, Tulsiram "establishes a system of knowledges and memories from within the Dalit lifeworlds,"*[3] *an*

[1]Sharmila Rege, *Writing Caste/Writing Gender: Reading Dalit Women's Testimonios* (Delhi: Zubaan, 2006), 13.

[2]Baby Kamble, *The Prisons We Broke* [Jina Amucha], trans. Maya Pandit (Hyderabad: Orient BlackSwan, 2008), 37.

[3]Judith Misrahi-Barak, K. Satyanarayana, and Nicole Thiara, eds., *Dalit Text: Aesthetics and Politics Re-imagined* (London: Routledge, 2020), 144.

archive of the cosmologies of the oppressed that takes seriously the thought of earlier generations.

In the fifteen years since its publication, Murdahiya *has achieved critical and popular acclaim. Doctoral dissertations and YouTube videos are dedicated to its exegesis. It has come to be regarded as a landmark text of Hindi literature, Dalit studies, and the social sciences, and it has been translated and published in German.*

The narrative of Murdahiya *spans the seventeen years from 1949 to 1966, from Tulsiram's birth to his flight from the village and completion of twelfth standard at a hostel for Dalit students in the district headquarters of Azamgarh. Except for the final chapter, the entire storyline takes place in Tulsiram's ancestral village of Dharampur, where he lives in a patrilineal joint family with his grandmother, parents, cousins, paternal uncles, and their wives. Education provides the book's structure. From the first paragraph's meditation on illiteracy to key transitions between chapters to the escape to the city, the narrative charts a sequence of extraordinary transformations made possible by Tulsiram's progress through school. But this framework only minimally determines the text, most of which lies beyond the classroom. The bulk of the story follows the people of Dharampur in their personal and collective grappling with landlords, witches, vultures, abductions, police, nomadic entertainers, drought, surfeit, the soil, and human and animal death. Often Tulsiram is witness to the central action rather than the protagonist.* Murdahiya *is as much the story of Nataniya, the dancer eager to learn English; Jogi Baba, the ascetic who speaks only in rhyme; Chintamani Singh, the generous and academically sluggish thakur's son; and Tulsiram's allegedly century-old grandmother with her buried hoard of British coins, as it is the story of the author himself.*

The irony of a New Delhi-based professor of international relations penning an extensive treatise on a single village in Uttar Pradesh is not lost on Tulsiram. His portrait of the village is devotedly local: alive to the distinguishing qualities of specific trees, ponds, fields, and dwellings, and committed to the preservation of vernacular turns of phrase and the unique speech styles of particular persons. At the same time and without compromising the richness of the sense of place, Tulsiram also indicates the many ways in which the world infiltrates the village and vice versa. A bonded laborer tells stories from his time with the British army in Baghdad, rumors of Nehru's death in far-off Delhi shock the village, uncles labor in the jute mills of distant Calcutta, and a communist leader from a neighboring district migrates to the Soviet Union. Movements between the village and the world increase as the story progresses, culminating in Tulsiram's own hijra to Azamgarh.

The selection presented here comes from the first two chapters of Murdahiya. *These opening pages introduce many of the dramatis personae that populate the book as a whole. Themes that pervade the autobiography find their first articulation here. The final section of chapter two, included here, describes a troubling event that occurs in the village death grounds, establishing the significance of the book's title. The selection, like the book as a whole, presents formidable challenges to the translator, foremost among them the rendering of the distance from the standard of dialect, especially in children's rhymes and the peculiarly poetic speech of ascetics. On the other hand, there are ways in which Tulsiram gives the task of translation an auspicious start. Reflecting his commitment to fidelity in representing the lives and words of the people of his childhood, Tulsiram frequently elaborates within his Hindi narrative on the meaning of vernacular terms that have yet to be entered into any dictionary (e.g., "the meat ... was called daangar"). In this sense,* Murdahiya *is a text that contains its own glossary, providing the translator and the reader, not to mention the social historian and linguist, a most unusual gift.*

ACKNOWLEDGMENT

I would like to thank Dr. Angira Chaudhary, daughter of Dr. Tulsiram, for her encouragement of this translation. My thanks also to the editors of *Mānoa* and of this special issue.

REFERENCES

Kamble, Baby. *The Prisons We Broke* [Jina Amucha]. Translated by Maya Pandit. Hyderabad: Orient BlackSwan, 2008.

Misrahi-Barak, Judith, K. Satyanarayana, and Nicole Thiara, eds. *Dalit Text: Aesthetics and Politics Re-Imagined.* London: Routledge, 2020.

Rege, Sharmila. *Writing Caste/Writing Gender: Reading Dalit Women's Testimonios.* Delhi: Zubaan, 2006.

Ignorance was my ancestral birthright. How many generations separate me from the first member of the human species to be my lineal forebear, I do not know. But not one of them was educated. Roughly twenty-three centuries ago, when Menander the Greek came to the subcontinent, he observed that the ordinary people of India have no knowledge of script and are thus unable to study. This did not bother his contemporaries, though modern Indian pandits lose no opportunity to refute and denounce Menander. The reality is that even today tens of millions of Indians testify to the soundness of the Greek's remark. The fruit of this millennium-old illiteracy is that the yoke of ignorance, with its companion blind belief, has never lifted from the shoulders of my ancestors.

We might begin with my grandfather. According to my father, a demon bludgeoned grandfather to death with a rod. Of five brothers, my father is the youngest. The story they all tell is that grandfather, whose name was Joothan—which means leftovers or despoiled food—went late one night to a bramble-choked pond in the jungle. Next to the pond was a small garden of peas that he used to cultivate. It was to protect this humble harvest from wild animals that he made the night excursion. In the moonlight he spied a creature called a saahi—a kind of porcupine—in the garden, eating the crop. Grandfather raised his lathi and attacked the creature. No sooner did the rod strike it than the saahi, assuming its fierce manifestation, outspread its mantle of enormous, bristling spikes—and disappeared. According to my family, the creature was not, in fact, a saahi, but rather a demon attached to that place. Grandfather returned home from the encounter, frightened. The tale of the demon swept through the village. Out of terror, everyone avoided the area near the pond. Everyone began to say that the demon would surely seek revenge.

Then one night when grandfather was sleeping in the granary, the saahi-disguised demon arrived with a lathi and beat him until he was a corpse. I never laid eyes on grandfather, as this supernatural homicide occurred years before my birth. His murder remains a knot of unanswered questions even now. The canons of logical reasoning suggest that a person in the locality—an enemy of my grandfather's—murdered him, obscuring the crime behind the collective psychological projection of the saahi-demon. Whatever the truth of the matter, this ghastly turn of events hurled every member of my family into a pit of terrified blind belief. As a result, our home became a center for the propitiation of Bhut Baba, lord of malevolent spirits. Ojhas and exorcists prospered. When anyone suffered so much as a headache, the incantations and broom beatings began. In such a bewitched environment, should a baby be born in a village called Dharampur in Azamgarh District on the first of July, 1949, what manner of birthright would he inherit?

Unsurprisingly, from early childhood itself I was stamped by the seal of superstition born of ignorance. My grandmother's name was Musariya. She lived more than a hundred years. The loose flesh that swung from her face and arms attested to her antiquity. People in the village said that grandmother had eaten crow meat, and this was why she did not die. Village wisdom held that those who consume crow's flesh increase their lifespan. In any case, grandmother used to say that on the third day of a certain lunar phase of a certain month, my father was born. This is why she named him Tesri, or Third. My mother's name was Dheerja, that is, Patience. My father was skilled at catching fish. He could catch them from any body of water, and that too with apparent ease. By the title Machharmarwa—Fish Killer—he achieved celebrity in the annals of the district. When people went anywhere to fish, they would plead with father to come with them and touch the water, as this ensured every person a full catch. Later my mother told me that immediately upon my birth, my father caught a fish from the local pond and buried it alive beneath the cot on which I was born. This was a kind of magical practice by means of which he believed that I, too, would one day obtain historical renown as Fish Killer. This was possibly the summit of my parents' highest ambitions, to see me crowned the next Machharmarwa of Perfected Hand. What higher aspirations, after all, befit a couple of Dalit field laborers?

Mother said that she had given birth to several children before me, but each one died within a short time. Thus, when I was born, my father took me in his lap to a place called Sherpur Kuti, a Shiva temple a kilometer and a half from the village, and pleaded with the priest, Baba Harihar Das, to bless me. Baba Harihar Das was a magnanimous soul. Blessing me to stay alive, he named me Tulsiram. Baba said that just as Tulsidas was a devotee of Ram, so this boy too would, as Tulsiram, grow up to be a devotee of Ram. In the process of keeping me alive, father himself became a staunch devotee of Shiva. He planted a new peepul tree by our home and conducted rites there. Every Saturday he ritually watered the peepul, and in the evenings he lit clay lamps filled with ghee. Whatever it was that he said in prayer to Shiva, it sounded like someone speaking and weeping at the same time. According to father, as the peepul grew, so likewise did I. At the same time my decrepit grandmother's attachment to me grew.

When I was three years old, a smallpox epidemic came to the village. I was struck with a particularly violent case. Soon I was at death's threshold. At home, prayers were made to all the local gods and goddesses. In the villages in those times, the Dalits had their own gods and goddesses, deities the savarna did not worship. In our village, Mother Chamariya and Father Deeh were two such deities worshipped by Dalits. Sacrifices of pigs and goats were made to them both. In addition to the sacrifice, they were offered halwa, fried cakes, "pujaura," and the libation of "dhaar." Nutmeg, cloves, and dates would be mixed in a pot of water—we called this "dhaar"—and a handful of barley grains was called "pujaura." The shrine of Mother

Chamariya was near that same bramble-choked pond next to grandfather's haunted pea garden. An array of clay elephants and horses, baked in the kilns of the Kumhars, stood there. The same kind of elephants and horses were placed at the shrine of Father Deeh, not far from the Brahmin quarter of the village. As I mentioned, my family also propitiated the demon, but unlike Mother Chamariya and Father Deeh, it had no designated shrine in the village. Some distance to the southwest of our village was another village called Daulatabad, and near that, in a desolate area, rose the vast canopy of an ancient peepul. According to my family, our demon lived there, in that tree. Thus we would trek to the venerable peepul to propitiate the spirit. Vows were also made to Mother Sheetala in hopes of recovering from smallpox. The Mother Sheetala temple was twenty kilometers to the northwest, near the small town of Nizamabad. Once a year the village's entire Dalit population made a pilgrimage, sacrificing piglets and offering halwa and fried cakes. To keep Mother Sheetala fully satisfied, prostitutes would be engaged for a dance performance. Women specializing in such dance were readily available near the temple.

Smallpox struck me with such severity that my family had largely given up hope of my survival. Apart from the vows and sacrifices to all the deities and spirits, there was no question of attempting any kind of medical treatment. With all the certitude of blind belief, my family firmly rejected the idea of taking medicine. In any case, smallpox was not curable at that time. My family understood it to be the affliction of Mother Sheetala. There was an exorcist from another village who used to do the rounds with his jhaad-phunk, muttering indecipherable mantras while breaking cloves and beating you with his "broom." Making a switch of the broken branches of neem trees along with their leaves, he would strike you with it all over the body. Meanwhile, my antique grandmother, the Dalit goddess's unshakable devotee, poured ghee into a dung cake fire and kept repeating, "Victory to Mother Chamariya, Victory to Mother Chamariya," keeping the sacred flame alive. My grandmother wept more than my mother. Finally, as the smallpox completed its cycle, I began to recover. My family declared with unbroken faith that it was their rites and prayers that kept me alive. Pigs, goats, and even a buffalo had been sacrificed in the fulfillment of their vows. My life was saved. No sooner had the smallpox receded, however, than the pitted scars of the disease settled all over my body. My face, in particular, became a warehouse of these lesions. In order to sift dirt and stones from grain, the metalsmiths of the village used to fashion thin strips of iron into a bowl-like shape and, with a small chisel, bore hundreds of little perforations into its base—this rough sieve was called an "akha." The exterior of the base of the akha would be jagged from the chisel's bores. My face looked like that outer part of the akha. The aspect of this whole smallpox episode that had the longest-reaching effect on my life, though, was that the vision in my right eye was extinguished. In India's society of blind belief, the one-eyed earn permanent membership in the registry of the "inauspicious." I too gained admission into that category at the precocious age of three. To one and all, both at home and in the world, I became an evil omen.

There were others in my village who also fell under the category of the inauspicious. One was an old Brahmin, the octogenarian Jangu Pandey. He lived his entire life unmarried. He had no one of his own. On his evening walks he would often stroll through the Dalit basti. In several families his arrival always sparked a commotion. People ordered their new daughters-in-law to stay indoors. They believed that if Jangu Pandey's glance fell on a family's daughter-in-law, misfortune would strike her—most likely, she would remain childless. One incident of this sort pains me to recall even now. Near our home stood a mango tree that used to flower spectacularly. One time Jangu Pandey turned up gazing at this mango tree because the blossoms were so appealing. My family members promptly spread the word that Jangu Pandey had laid the evil eye on the tree. It would no longer bear fruit. Later, in fact, it bore plenty of fruit.

Similarly, in our village there was an elderly Brahmin woman whose name no one knew. She was simply called "Panditain." The Panditain was a childless widow. People disliked seeing her, too. Throughout the village people said that if you came before the Panditain, you would fail at any venture. If anyone embarked on some errand and happened to cross paths with the Panditain, that person would return home and wait an interval for the inauspiciousness to dissipate. Only later would they again set out on their venture. Although Jangu Pandey and the Panditain addressed people with exceptional courtesy, on account of these beliefs, they were regularly and without reason treated with disrespect.

Five years had elapsed since India's independence—that is, the year 1952 was approaching its end—when I joined the ranks of evil omens and the inauspicious. I was three years old. Sympathies born of the rural environment gradually began to stir in my brain. My father was the youngest of five brothers. We were a joint family; young and old, about fifty of us lived together. Father's middle brother, the third in line in terms of seniority, was a man of ferocious temper and cruel disposition. Without provocation anyone could become the target of his coarse abuse. He had two sons—my cousins—who were perfect replicas of his cruelty. They would often call me "Kanwa Kanwa"—the One-Eyed. Now and then others would call me this at home as well. No one, in any case, told them not to. Even my mother, in the face of their viciousness, would fall into a weepy silence.

My grandmother's unwavering attachment to me strengthened day by day. I was the smallest member of that teeming extended family. At night grandmother put me to sleep next to her, steadily stroking my face with her hand and praying to Mother Chamariya. As I grew, my disgrace and inauspiciousness grew with me. Later, when I began to understand things, grandmother told me that before the smallpox, on account of my being the youngest, everyone in the family competed to hold me in their laps and play with me, but that after the disease everything had changed. Father's cut-heart middle brother's name was Laggar. If he got angry with anyone in the house, he immediately stopped eating and drinking. In his own fashion he was a Gandhian, constantly undertaking hunger strikes. If any family member, seeking to placate him, brought a plate of food or tumbler of water, that person would be drenched in a torrent of insults. Laggar Uncle would knock over the dish—food and all—and then shatter the plate by hurling the tumbler at it. In those days people in the village had dishes of cheap bell-metal or tin alloy that would break into pieces if struck. At least one plate in this way fell victim to my uncle's every rage. Over the years, who knows how many dishes sacrificed their phenomenal existence to his temper. Everyone lived in terror of him. His two sons were the lawful heirs of this terror. The father and sons together, when they were in a jovial mood, would call me over and play a game. They had me cover up my one good eye and ask me to count how many fingers they were waving in front of me. With my afflicted eye I could only make out vague, misty shapes, but on that basis I would guess, and they would be amused. As a sign of their gratification, they would congratulate me: "Sharp little One-Eye." I, too, was pleased when I correctly discerned their fingers. I thought myself a great mathematician. But when I grew a little older, I realized that this counting act was in fact ridicule for my cousins' entertainment. Gradually the game lost its pleasure for me. It became an anguished exercise, but I could not muster the courage to refuse the foggy finger count. This went on for years. I can now say that the pain born of the half-blind counting ordeal gave me my first awareness of interior suffering. It was later that I became conscious of the pain born of being an evil omen. These sufferings suffused my early childhood, and at a tender age I became unusually sensitive.

My grandparents and their forebears were bonded laborers in the fields of the Brahmin landlords of the village. It was these landlords who had given my grandparents small garden plots. The village's other Dalits, too, worked the fields of these same landlords. The ploughman's bond was handed down from generation to generation. In my family, my father's four older brothers did not work as agricultural laborers because out of their several grown sons, five worked in the coalfields of Asansol and the jute mills and iron factories of Calcutta. But my father never escaped the ancestral ploughman's bond. He would often say that if he left off tilling the soil, he would incur the sin of brahmahatya, Brahmin murder. Being fanatically religious, he felt the ploughman's bond was both his birthright and sacred duty. My mother, too, toiled as a field laborer. My family was like an ethnological museum filled with various kinds of people displaying all manner of customs and life-styles. Father's eldest brother, called Sommar, was the chosen Chaudhuri of the Chamars of twelve villages. How deep into India's premodern history goes the tradition of the twelve villages of eastern Uttar Pradesh Chamars, no one knows, but the Chamars do in fact have a vast panchayat, said to consist of twelve villages, from which a grand committee elects a single Chaudhuri. In practice the Chaudhuri acquires the powers of a kind of judge. Chamars of the "twelve villages" bring before the Chaudhuri any internal dispute that arises among them. The panchayat is then solemnly summoned, and after long hours of collective head kneading, the Chaudhuri delivers his final verdict, which is regarded by all as authoritative with immediate effect.

Of the problems brought before the Chaudhuri of twelve villages, two kinds were resolved in a very peculiar way. One was the development of sexual relations between a young woman of the village and some man or her becoming pregnant out of wedlock. The other was the consumption by a Chamar of the meat of dead cattle—cows, buffaloes, or oxen. A noteworthy fact on this carrion-eating issue is that in our region, before independence, when cows or oxen or buffaloes would die, all the Chamars would eat the meat. My old grandmother, when she would put me to sleep, often shared recollections of the world of her childhood—wondrous, fascinating stories. Considering that grandmother lived to a hundred, these recollections most likely described the 1860s and 1870s. I listened to her narratives with rapt attention. In one of her recollections, grandmother told me that when she married and came to our village, she learned that when any cow, buffalo, or ox died in the village, it was brought into the nearby jungle, its hide was removed, and then with hatchets and knives, all the Dalits would chop up the carcass, fill bamboo baskets with the meat, and take it home. For the most part it was women who carved the meat. Grandmother also said that whenever a Chamar man began to remove the animal's hide, the vultures would appear, hundreds of them, encircling the place. Dogs by the dozen turned up barking. Jackals, too, would arrive, but seeing the dogs and the women at work, they watched from a distance. Vicious competition broke out between the women, the dogs, and the vultures over the distribution of meat. Grandmother herself took part in these contests. By necessity she would immediately cook a portion of the meat she brought home, but most of the raw flesh she would hang out to dry in hot sunlight. After thoroughly drying it, she would store the meat in a vessel of unbaked clay. By this process she accumulated a storehouse of dried meat, and in the lean months when no other food was available, the family would sate its hunger by finding various ways to cook this dried beef. The meat of dead cattle was called "daangar."

After Independence, the Chamars launched a campaign to end the eating of daangar. It was highly successful. It is widely considered that Baba Saheb Ambedkar spearheaded this campaign, but in our twelve villages no one knew of Ambedkar, whereas Jagjivan Ram was quite popular. Despite the success of the anti-carrion campaign, in villages here and there people continued to eat daangar on the sly. But if they were caught, their case would be brought before the Chaudhuri. My oldest uncle, Sommar, had been elected Chaudhuri sometime before Independence. He had a penchant for long-winded disputation; thus, he was made Chaudhuri for life. There was logic in his arguments and impartiality as well, so calls to replace him never arose in the twelve villages. Whenever a controversy arose in the twelve villages, the panchayat would assemble in front of our home. People would sit on the large stone platform surrounding the well. As representatives of all the twelve villages came for the panchayat, the crowd was impressive. The panchayat commenced with a leisurely round of ganja smoking and a long tour of the hookah. In our family alone there were ten high-level ganja connoisseurs. In the evening everyone would smoke ganja, which I would light for them again and again with a knot of straw. Having ignited the knot, I would place it, blazing and glowing red, on the ganja-filled chillum. I was around five years old when I secured permanent employment as the ganja lighter. I hated the task, but what to do. The primary reason for my hatred was that any kind of smoke caused me to choke. Later in life this was diagnosed as an allergy. On days when the panchayat met, straw-burning duty seemed to never end. On account of this duty, I was compelled to observe the proceedings of the panchayat until the very end.

As I have said, disputes regarding sexual liaisons and carrion eating were dealt with in a curious way by the panchayat. With sexual relations, the entire family of the young woman concerned would be declared "outcaste." This meant no one would give them water or share the hookah; they were fully boycotted by the entire twelve villages. No one could as much as speak to the family. The way the boycott was announced was itself very strange. In the twelve villages someone or another was almost always getting married or having some occasion for a collective meal. The person who was to be declared outcaste would be invited to take part in one of these collective meals. He would sit in a row with everybody else. He would be served food on a leaf plate like everybody else. But at the moment that this person took food in his hand and raised it toward his mouth, suddenly another person seized his wrist. Then everyone present told him, in unison, that he had been declared outcaste and therefore was forbidden to eat. Having been declared outcaste, the man would return to his home in disgrace. This was how boycotts began. Later, if the outcaste individual wanted to return to the brotherhood, he would appeal to the twelve villages. The panchayat would be summoned, and, as a form of penance, a date would be fixed for the offender to treat the entire caste to a feast of pork and rice. If, in the meantime, the unwed young woman got pregnant, then the women of the village who were experienced in delivering babies would press her belly in the cruelest manner to induce an abortion. Then on the appointed day, as the panchayat members were being served pork and rice, with the Chaudhuri's blessing, the girl would be doused with water from the Ganges and declared pure. After this, the outcaste family would make an appeal to the panchayat to vacate their crime. With one voice, the assembly would call out, "Bola Bola Sitaram," after which they declared the transgression forgiven. With that, the individual and family were readmitted to the brotherhood. In the matter of eating daangar, the same rite of expiation was adopted. In smaller disputes, the guilty party would be told to pay penance by providing the community with the long rugs on which people sat for collective meals or giant brass and bell-metal cauldrons for preparing wedding feasts. Such supplies would be kept at the home of the Chaudhuri or some other community member, and when an occasion arose anyone could make use of them. When the occasion was over, the supplies would be returned. In the 1950s panchayats like these enjoyed high repute among the Dalits, but in the 1960s such traditions began to fade. Today the Chaudhuries of that era are nowhere to be seen, nor is there any sign of such panchayats.

My father's second brother was named Munessar, while the third brother was the angry one, Laggar. These two were both gurus in the Shivnarayan Panth, a religious order famous in Uttar Pradesh. Both "gurus" had dozens of disciples spread across far-flung villages. From our own village, as chance would have it, they had not a single disciple. Uncle Munessar was employed in a jute mill in Calcutta. Thus, his disciples were also there, though they were all originally from Uttar Pradesh. In the Shivnarayan Panth, whenever disciples met their guru, they had a peculiar way of greeting them. First, they tied turbans to their heads and then squatted with bent knees and flat heels in front of the guru. Joining their hands, they would reach out and touch the guru's feet. Moving their heads left and right in yogic manner, they would then rest their heads on the guru's feet and say loudly, "Allegiance, Sahib!" When the gurus visited the homes of their disciples, their feet would be washed in a dish, and the disciples would drink the dirty water. In our home, in keeping with the Shivnarayan Panth's tradition, there were three festivals every year when disciples would be present in numbers. These three occasions fell on the days of Holi, Diwali, and Krishna Janamashtami. The gatherings on these days were called Seating the Sovereign. A low-legged wooden platform would be set up in the manner of an altar. Clean fabric would be spread over the surface, and on it would be placed the glass-encased image of whatever god or goddess was conveniently available. Bundles of incense sticks would be lit. Although no one in our family was literate, we kept in our home a handwritten manuscript—who knows in what language—wrapped in red cloth and called the Anyaas. No one could so much as touch this manuscript. This mysterious Anyaas, too, was placed on the altar. This is what was called Seating the Sovereign. As soon as the text was in place, the guru and his disciples would all simultaneously sit around the platform, and with dhol and tambourine and other musical instruments, a night-long performance of Shivnarayan devotional songs would commence. Kabir songs, too, were sung now and then. At the same time milk, ghee, semolina, jaggery, raisins, and other ingredients were cooked together in a giant cauldron, making prasad that would be distributed at the end of the festival. When a member of the Shivnarayan Panth died, his corpse was not burned like a Hindu; rather, he was buried like a Muslim. Every now and then a corpse would be set afloat in the Ganges instead. A special feature of the last rites was that as the deceased was carried from home to cemetery, the processors would sing devotional songs with drums and cymbals, and five times along the way would halt, set the corpse on the ground, and sing a particular Shivnarayan hymn called The Moth. At the grave the singing and drumming accelerated, and as the body was lowered into the ground, the musicians reached a furious tempo. Three days later all the processors gathered at the home of the deceased and ate oven-roasted wheat grain and drank sharbat. This wheat grain was called "bahuri." A fascinating detail about "bahuri" is that when Dalit women in the village quarreled, they would abuse one another as their son's or husband's or father's "bahuri bhujane," which was considered extremely offensive. As "bhujane" is one who causes others to eat and bahuri is the grain eaten at funerals, "bahuri bhujane" meant someone who desired her own family member's death. Later, on the thirteenth day after death, a huge feast would be held. The biggest specialty of the Shivnarayan Panth is this: its founder was a kshatriya of Uttar Pradesh's Baliya District, but his following came entirely from the Dalit community. That this order's leadership is entirely in Dalit hands is itself a little-known fact. The person who becomes head of the Shivnarayan Panth is called the Gurumukh.

Father's fourth older brother was named Munnar. He was utterly unlike my other uncles—the Chaudhuri of twelve villages or either of the Shivnarayan Panth gurus. This uncle was a collaborative, unifying kind of person. On account of this quality, he was made head of the family. He maintained the accounts for whatever little the family acquired beyond immediate needs. Munnar Uncle believed deeply in ghosts and devils. Like grandmother, he was a devotee of Mother Chamariya. Every year in the hot season all the Dalits of the village held the "pujaiya" of Mother Chamariya and Father Deeh. This pujaiya was different from ordinary worship. Munnar Uncle played the leading role in organizing the annual pujaiya. He collected contributions from everyone in the village for the event. Late in the night, people congregated in an open field outside the village and began preparing dhaar in large earthen pots. The obligatory exorcist or tantric who was invited would make the rounds, breaking cloves and repeating names of goddesses in eerie, halting speech. This continued for hours, long into the desolation of the night. Next to the pots brimming with dhaar, little makeshift flags of red fabric were planted, and near these was placed an enormous round gourd called a bhatua. The interior of the bhatua is vivid red. Cut into it, and it looks like a bloodbath. When the exorcist completed his rites, Munnar Uncle led the people in raising the pots of dhaar onto their shoulders. They gathered the red flags. The procession began, with Munnar

Uncle in the lead, holding the giant bhatua aloft. With loud collective cries of "Victory to Mother Chamariya and Father Deeh," the procession wound its way in the darkness to the boundary of another village, where there was a crossroads. Raising the bhatua into the air, uncle then hurled it to the ground, shattering the gourd into crimson fragments. Dhaar was poured from the pots onto the earth. The red flags were buried. In silence, the people then returned to their homes. The destruction of the bhatua in the pujaiya is probably a symbol of human sacrifice. The villagers had steadfast faith that completing the annual pujaiya would ensure that in the following year, neither sickness nor disaster would befall the village.

On the second day of pujaiya, the people of the Dalit basti collectively bought a large pig and offered it in sacrifice. The means of acquiring the victim was fascinating. The people who raised swine lived in distant villages. Among Dalits it was typically the Pasi caste that reared pigs. No Pasi lived in our village. Here and there were villages that had one or two Pasi homes. To keep pigs, one needed to dig a ten- to fifteen-foot-wide, two-foot-deep rectangular pit, build a five-foot-high wall around its perimeter, and over this hang a covering of woven sugarcane leaves. The entrance to this structure was extremely narrow, and the interior low. This dwelling, which would house some fifteen or twenty pigs, was called a "khobhaar." The swine only came into the khobaar at night. Their days they spent wandering here and there in the village and nearby, searching for food. Thus someone who sought to acquire a pig had first to pursue the drove on their peregrinations in order to make a selection. Once the victim was selected and the price settled, the chase began. This was an hours-long, community-wide marathon. Sometimes the pig would elude its captors an entire afternoon. So long as it kept running, the pursuit continued. Ultimately, with great difficulty, the pig would be surrounded and captured.

After capture, the pig's four legs would be tied together with thick rope. Inserting a sturdy bamboo staff, four men would hoist the staff on their shoulders with the pig hanging from it. They would then carry their prize—two in front, two behind, the way Kahaars carry a palanquin—back to their village. Just as daughters of the upper castes, when leaving their natal family upon marriage, sit weeping in the palanquin that carries them to the home of their husbands, so these sacrificial pigs, swinging upside down from the staff carried on men's shoulders, wail throughout the journey. The method of killing the pig for sacrifice was quite inhumane. Laying the creature on the ground and putting the bamboo staff on its neck and waist, four men would press down on it, while a fifth took a two-foot-long, sharply pointed iron rod called a "hikna" and plunged it into the pig's heart. At this moment the pig let out a terrifying shriek. The sound could be heard from miles away. The men joined the pig's mortal cry with exultations of victory to Mother Chamariya and Father Deeh. As soon as the pig died, the hikna was removed, and in its place a stick of the arhar bush of just the same length—called a "rahttha"—was inserted into the wound so that blood would not escape. The dead creature's bristles were removed, and its body was thoroughly roasted over burning sugarcane leaves to remove the roots of the hair. Then the "tail" was carved out—a solid one-kilo cut of rump meat, including the tail itself. This whole portion was specially reserved for the Chaudhuri of twelve villages. Whenever a pig was sacrificed in our village, or even just butchered without sacrifice, this tail portion would freely be sent to our home in the name of the Chaudhuri, my uncle. The remaining meat was portioned and purchased by each family according to necessity. The tail portion signified the special status of Chaudhuri Uncle in the twelve villages and the esteem given to his Solomonic role. This tradition continued through Chaudhuri Uncle's entire life.

Taken as a whole, then, my family was not only an exceptionally large specimen of the patrilineal joint family system. It was truly a house of wonders: a museum containing demons and ghosts, gods and goddesses, property and poverty, dignity and debasement, auspiciousness and inauspiciousness, justice and iniquity, truth and falsehood, envy, spite, pleasure, suffering, and so on. The one thing it did not contain was education.

In those days a revolutionary development took place in our centuries-old family. This was 1954, and I had reached the age of about five. Those members of our family who worked in the coalfields of Asansol and the mills of Calcutta periodically sent us postcards. In our Dalit basti there was not a soul who could read them. Only Brahmins in the village were educated. When we requested them to read these postcards aloud to us, they either turned a deaf ear or prefaced the reading with degrading remarks. Piqued by the Brahmins' behavior, my household turned its attention inward, to the youngest child in the family, and bestowed its favor upon me. In the classroom adjacent to the aforementioned Shiva temple, with the mission of deciphering postcards, I was sent to school.

***

Before taking me to school, of course, father had to consult Amika Pandey to determine the "sait," the most auspicious date for me to begin. Amika Pandey was famous in our village for discerning the auspicious moment for everything from marriages to sowing crops to harvesting. The secret of his knowledge was a book that he possessed, a foot tall and half as wide, called a "patra." This he sacramentally wrapped in red cloth. He permitted no one—not even his family members—to touch it, such was the power of its arcane mysteries. It was said among Dalits in the village that Amika Pandey's patra was delivered to earth from the divine realm by Lord Brahma himself. Amika Pandey could predict the dates of lunar and solar eclipses. Naturally, when the eclipses occurred on the dates he foretold, people were astonished at his miraculous prescience. To determine a "sait,"

Amika Pandey would open his patra to a page seemingly at random and, with his eyes closed, move his middle finger here and there before stopping on some particular place; whatever day was written beneath his finger was declared the auspicious day. Among the Dalits who witnessed these things, a firm conviction took hold that Amika Pandey's book contained the entirety of Vedic and Puranic knowledge. The reality behind these wonders was that Pandey's famous patra was an almanac published once a year by a Varanasi printing press. This almanac published the dates of lunar eclipses, solar eclipses, and all the Hindu festivals and holidays for the year to come. With the aid of this talisman, Amika Pandey determined that the date of my commencing school would be a Tuesday. By the Hindu calendar it was the month of Asadh.

The first day of school I remember well because my father carried me there on his shoulders. The school, adjacent to the aforementioned Shiva shrine, was called Primary Pathshala, Sherpur Kuti. There was a stream across the path about a kilometer and a half from our village and a furlong before the school. This frequently flooded in the monsoon, creating difficulties for the students. My father was an unusually generous kind of person. Every year when he took me to school during the monsoon floods, he would remain by the swollen stream and carry a dozen children across, one at a time, on his shoulders. This quality made him quite popular among my classmates. And not only them. Three of the five teachers in the school came from villages six or seven miles from the school on our side of the stream. Now and then when the waters reached chest level, in the same way he did the children, father would carry these teachers across on his shoulders as well. Especially in the evening when it was flooded, several students and these three teachers would wait on the far side of the stream for my father to transport them—and he reliably did so. Other students crossed a bridge over the same stream about a kilometer and a half away from the school to get home to their far-flung villages.

When I arrived in this manner at school for the first time, the teacher, Munshi Ramsurat Lal, wrote my name in the register and asked father when I was born. The reply: four or five years back, in the rainy season. Munshi-ji converted this on the spot to the First of July, 1949, the date that has been yoked to my birth ever since. Given their illiteracy, there was no norm among Dalits in those days of documenting birth dates or horoscope; most parents linked their children's birth to the season. This is why teachers of that era would write July First upon hearing "rainy season," January First on hearing "winter," and March First on hearing "hot season." This is the formula in no small number of villages in India even today. As a result, most Dalits in government service retire on these three dates. In those days it was the practice to register all the students on the first day of school itself. In my first class there were forty-three students, three of them girls. We were seated on mats on the floor with our classmates by roll-call number. The first row began with number one on the roster and ended with number thirteen. The remaining two rows had fifteen students each. My name fell in the first row, fifth position. Of the thirteen in that row, there were, besides me, Chikhuri, Ramjhu, Baburam, Yadunath, Mulku, Ramker, Dalsingar, Jaggan, Ramnath, Birju, Babulal, and Mewa. The secret of the thirteen quickly came to light. We were all Dalit. In the presence of Munshi-ji, no other child touched us. This was the environment in which my education began.

On the first day of class Munshi-ji taught us that when we were called for attendance, we should stand and call out, "Present, Munshi-ji!" Next we were instructed to stand and raise the pinky finger of our right hand if we should need to urinate. In the beginning most children were unable to pronounce the word "present" properly, inviting a shower of abuse from Munshi-ji. He directed his anger especially toward Dalit children, whom he called "Chamarkit." Over minor mistakes he would have students collect thick stalks of arhar pulse, bundle them into a switch, and fiercely whip their palms with it, hurling insults all along. The terror of Munshi-ji spread among the students in the very first year of school. At this time the practice of writing on paper was almost completely absent at the primary school level. Only in the fifth standard were students able to use paper to some extent. Until then, students did all of their reading and writing on wooden tablets. These tablets, about fifteen inches high and nine inches wide, were first carved by the village blacksmith using an adze and then polished smooth with a plane. But in order to make the surface suitable for writing, students would every day blacken it with their "pochara," dry it in the sun, and then rub it again with a "chulla" until it gleamed. After this, it could be written upon by a sharpened reed dipped in a chalky white mixture. The method for making pochara was quite interesting. Every child at home would prop up a "parai," or shallow clay saucer, just above the flame of a small kerosene lamp; after an hour or so a good quantity of residue would accumulate there. This lampblack would be collected and mixed in a clay pot, and the result was called pochara. "Chulla" was the tool with which the tablet was rubbed after the pochara was applied. To learn mathematics, every student had to bring from home white, one-foot-high stalks of jute and color them red, green, blue, and yellow. These stalks were called "lagga" or "santha." These, then, were what I possessed in the name of school supplies in the first standard: one wooden tablet, one container of chalk mixture, one reed "pen," one pot of pochara or lampblack, one chulla, and these multi-colored jute stalks. There were, however, no books. With these materials commenced my revolutionary campaign to acquire the capacity to read postcards.

Munshi-ji wrote letters on the blackboard and told the students to imitate them on our tablets. In the beginning, whenever I picked up the reed to write, my hands trembled from fear, and my every effort to produce a letter failed. On top of this, Mushi-ji's "Chamarkit" abuse inspired such terror that ultimately at the very mention of going to school, I would burst into tears. On these occasions father would beat me and drag me to school, saying in his rustic dialect that if I didn't learn, who would read the postcards? But my heart was not at all in my studies. Thus, compared with other children in my class, I was slow to learn to write ka, kha, ga, gha, and so on, and that too with the help of my classmate Sankatha Singh. Sankatha Singh was the son of a prominent kshatriya landlord in Bari village, about three kilometers east of our village. He and I were roughly equal in age, about five or six, but he was more worldly and of a compassionate disposition. He learned to write very quickly. At that time the practice of untouchability was extremely widespread in schools as elsewhere, and savarna students generally did not socialize with their Dalit classmates. But Sankatha Singh was an exception. He always talked with me. It was he who, after a fashion, compelled me to learn to write. Rather than Munshi-ji, it was Sankatha Singh who was the more successful first-year educator in my case. With confidence he drilled me on the alphabet, making me draw the characters over and over. When all my writing depleted the chalk mixture, I would dilute the remainder with some drops of water in order to continue. This made the chalk thin and my letters illegible. To make this diluted chalk thick again, Sankatha Singh taught me a rhyming mantra, which we would then chant together. This was the mantra: "When pond water makes thin, a kilo of chalk come in!" Sankatha Singh and I would chant this so-called mantra, reaching our hands toward our classmates' containers of chalk, clasping our hands as though capturing something, and then moving our hands back toward our own chalk containers. We would repeat the process over and over, believing that now our chalk mixture would have thickened. Soon all the students learned the mantra. Sometimes fights broke out when one student would accuse another of theft by chalk mantra. Some students even brought their allegations of magical chalk robbery before the court of Munshi-ji. This, of course, triggered our teacher's proclivity for abusive language, and an eruption of obscenity ensued. In any case, the mantra for thickening the chalk mixture supplied endless entertainment for us children. Chanting the mantra, we progressed from first to second standard. To proceed from first to second standard, Munshi-ji took from each student a two-rupee "passkarayi," that is, a bribe for passing. I obtained these two rupees from home with great difficulty. All the teachers took this passkarayi, and any student that did not give it was failed for the year. It was the norm in our school that each teacher taught a cohort of students continuously from the first to the fourth standard. After fourth, the same sequence from first standard began again. Fifth standard was always taught by the Headmaster. There were thus five teachers at our school: besides Munshi Ramsurat Lal, there were Vamshi Pandey, Hari Singh, Balram Singh, and Headmaster Parshuram Singh.

In third standard, my family refused to pay the two-rupee "passkarayi." Consequently, Munshi-ji failed me. When this news reached Balram Singh, whom everyone called Babu Sahib, he gave Munshi-ji a proper scolding. The reason for this was that by third standard I had become the top student in the school. I was especially interested in math. Every year games and competitions were held on the fifteenth of August and the twenty-sixth of January. One was the "math race." Students from second to fifth year took part in this contest. Facing a hundred-yard track, the students were asked a complex math problem. Whatever student could both solve the problem and reach the far end fastest would win first prize. The question's answer had to be solved in the mind alone, without the use of any kind of writing, and delivered verbally. In the math race I won first prize every year, on account of which the teachers were pleased with me. This was why Babu Sahib Balram Singh chastised Munshi-ji for failing me in third standard, and Munshi-ji, after a month, switched the fail to pass and admitted me into fourth. But for ten days or so Munshi-ji kept up a steady grumble about not getting his two rupees.

The reality is that for children in my circumstances in those days, to obtain two rupees was a bitter struggle. My family members said with contempt: what is the point of sending him to school if he can only pass by giving money? They assumed I must be weak in my studies to have failed the exam, which is why I had to pay the passkarayi. They could not believe that the passkarayi was a kind of bribe that every student had to pay without regard to their aptitude. Although in those days, like now, the government discounted the school fees of Dalit students, I still had to give two paisa every month. For the savarna children, the monthly fee was four annas. The currency of present-day India was not in circulation in those days. We had the rupee, the anna, and the paisa from the time of British rule. Coins were one paisa, half anna, one anna, two annas, four annas, eight annas, and one rupee. They were stamped with the face of the queen or king of England. In paper currency, there were the one, two, five, ten, and hundred rupee notes. There were two kinds of paisa coins. One, the same size as today's fifty-paisa coin, was made of copper and had a round hole at the center; in the village we called this a "chhedhava." The other paisa was as large as today's rupee coin, also made of copper, but with no hole; this was called a "double." Among Dalits it was considered highly auspicious to string together chhedhava coins and tie them around the waist of a newborn baby. Similarly auspicious was the amulet that people hung around children's necks, made by stringing thick thread through four-anna coins to which a goldsmith had attached hooks. Half-anna, one-anna, and two-anna coins were made of gilt, silver, and other metals. The silver one-rupee coin, which bore Queen Victoria's image, was wider, thicker, and heavier than today's equivalent. The Dalits of our village called this coin "Bistoria." Old people hoarded these bistorias and buried them beneath their homes; sometimes these persons died without having told anyone, and their stash remained hidden in the earth for years. Now and then you would hear about someone digging a new foundation after a house collapsed and finding an earthen jar of these coins. Sometimes the jar would contain silver or gold ornaments as well. In the quest for such buried treasure, a few people, under the influence of a local exorcist or tantric, would go so far as to sacrifice their own child. Even today stories of this kind appear in the newspapers sometimes.

My old grandmother possessed thirty-seven of these bistorias. Who knows how many years she had hidden the trove. I was the only one to whom she told the secret. A number of times she whispered in my ear how my grandfather—the one murdered by the demon—had collected the coins over the years and given them to her, one by one, to conceal. Grandmother told me that this all took place in the time of the Rangrez. By this she actually meant the English (Angrez) rather than the Cloth Dyers (Rangrez). Grandmother kept these thirty-seven coins in a small, jar-shaped clay vessel called a "bharuki." For a long time she buried this bharuki under a corner of the house. Then, in 1957, when I was studying in third standard, grandmother fell ill. She was struck by the kind of severe fever we called "jarhans." She took a spade and began digging in the earth, having posted me at the door to warn her if anyone was coming, as she did not want anyone to witness the excavation. Ultimately the bistoria-filled little bharuki emerged. Conspiratorially, she told me to count the coins. On a "leva"—a piece of bedding stitched together from old and torn-up fabrics—she placed all of the coins in an array, having me pick them up one by one to count. After each number I uttered, she took the coin from my hand and slipped it back into the bharuki so carefully that no passerby could perceive a jingle or clink. By this process we completed the inventory. The number thirty-seven was entirely foreign to grandmother's experience. For a long while she was incredulous. She knew well how to count from one to ten. Beyond this she went directly to twenty, thirty, forty, fifty, and one hundred. She understood these units in this fashion: she called ten "two fives," twenty "two tens," forty "two twenties," fifty "two twenties and one ten," and a hundred "two fifties." But thirty-seven was incomprehensible. Only with great difficulty, when I described it as "three short of two twenties," was the puzzle of thirty-seven resolved.

Grandmother then slept each night with her head resting on the bharuki, wrapped in an old rag and concealed beneath her bedroll. Almost every day of her illness, she told me that she planned to bequeath the stash to me. She made me swear by Mother Chamariya that I would tell no one. Daily when no one else was present, she would make me count the bistorias by that same old method, at the end of which she would say, "Three short of two twenties, no?" When I confirmed the number, she would momentarily beam with gratification, then repeat her command: "Tell no one." The limitless love and trust that grandmother lavished on me churned my soul. I worried about her illness. She kindled the sacred fire, poured libations to our village goddess Mother Chamariya, and muttered prayers, while I, sitting with her, silently prayed, "O Mother Chamariya! Take my life instead, don't let grandmother die." Imagining her imminent death, I was overcome with sadness and thought of her "ghuntu-muntu." Ghuntu-muntu was a game in which grandmother, lying on the ground, would seat me upon her bent knees and swing me back and forth, singing a children's rhyme: "The queen and king went out, the lake is a great big spout, tamarind trees round the lake, thirty-two eggs and a snake, Ramchander breaks his wand, the wand falls into the pond, fish eat it and grow, caw-caw says the crow, the tomcat pounces, the hyena's leg bounces, now get in the boat and row!" At the end of the story-rhyme, grandmother would cry out "Lala pala!" and, seating me on her lower legs, toss me into the air. All the children delighted in the ghuntu-muntu game. Another little story sung to pacify crying children went like this: "Bitter bitter crow, Nepal is full of snow, move on to Delhi, follow your belly, you silly crow you silly crow." Grandmother sang this one to me as well. [...]

Beyond these songs and games, there was a habit of grandmother's that I remembered vividly as her condition worsened. Whenever something like a guava or a sweet from the mithai shop showed up at our house, she would take some portion of it, hide it in a niche in the wall, and later feed it to me. In the wintertime, for example, she would roast a potato or some fresh pea pods on the fire, conceal it from the older children, and then give it to me to eat. Now grandmother's fever was gradually worsening. My family began talking about obtaining a shroud and other death preparations. Amid all this, a "hinguhara"—an itinerant vendor of asafoetida—came through the village. The specialty of this hinguhara was that in his travels across innumerable villages spread over a vast territory, he would arrive in each village precisely once a year and provide asafoetida to whomever needed it, noting their name and address in an ancient ledger that he carried with him. Taking no fee, he would then disappear. One year later, in the same month, he would return to the village, stand before his old customer's home, and deliver a request for payment in song. This manner of collecting his fee was highly appealing. Imagine there was a customer named Jagalu who took some asafoetida a year earlier; the hinguhara would now stand before his door and sing, "O mother of Jagalu, kindly set aside labors, repay asafoetida favors." He repeated the melody before each customer's home. By chance, on this day he arrived in front of our home with his collection song. The hinguhara's voice reached grandmother's ears. In a faint voice she told her sons to bring the asafoetida-man his payment, then fell silent. Munnar Uncle was head of the household. He went out and delivered the fee. Surprised, the hinguhara asked Munnar Uncle where grandmother was, since on every other occasion it was she who paid him. When he learned that grandmother was ill, he came in to see her and, seeing her condition, told Munnar Uncle to take her to the hospital immediately, otherwise she would die. In those days, about seven kilometers from our village, near the small market of Barahlganj, there was a two-room hospital staffed by one doctor of modern medicine. This doctor was known throughout the region as "the English doctor." It was at the advice of the asafoedita man that my family, for the very first time, rose above their superstition to take grandmother to the hospital. They repurposed a sagging old charpoy called a "jhilanga," lashing new rope and inserting bamboo poles along the sides to improvise a litter on which they laid grandmother down and carried her, two men in front and two behind, the seven kilometers to the hospital.

The doctor gave grandmother an injection with a large needle, a glass of red-colored solution to drink, and some small white pills to consume. On the same patched-up charpoy, she was then immediately carried home again, and in three or four days, she began to recover. I was overjoyed. Grandmother was rescued from death, and a few days later she again buried the bistoria-filled bharuki in the earth. Perhaps this re-interring of her treasure was, for grandmother, a rite of renewal, a kind of recommitment to life.

When I think of the village, I always think of that hinguhara. No one knew his name or where he lived. Even when someone asked, he revealed nothing. He wore a dhoti, kurta, and a Gandhi cap perched at a rakish angle. He also had an enormous belly, which suited well the overall look. In appearance you would think he was the older brother of the senior Congress politician Sitaram Kesri. For children in the village, one of the best evening entertainments throughout the year was to stand in front of someone or another's house and, imitating the hinguhara's voice, loudly sing, "Repay asafoetida favors," and then run away. The one time in the year when the hinguhara turned up in the village, dozens of children would follow him from house to house and take immense pleasure in his collection song. The hinguhara carried a small hand-sewn satchel over his shoulder. In this he stored his asafoetida supply and the kind of paper used to wrap puris. He also kept his collected fees in this little bag. The hinguhara's magic satchel was just like the kind carried by the ochre-clad ascetics who wandered from village to village playing the sarangi and asking for alms. There was a jogi—an ascetic of this kind—who came to our village once a year. First, he would make a complete round of every corner of the village, filling the air with his sarangi melodies and exquisite song. Then he returned to every house one by one, accepting alms from each. Like the asafoetida-man, this ascetic was beloved in the village. We also had our own jogi, the ascetic who lived among us. By caste he was a Noniya, a salt-maker. He was not the kind of jogi who wore ochre robes, nor did he beg for alms. People on their own brought him food rations. He would wrap a white dhoti or lungi around his waist, tie both sides together, and then drape the garment down from his neck. He wore nothing else. His beard and hair hung down his body almost as long. In his hand he always carried a "tumri"—the sadhu's vessel, a dried hollow gourd with a hanging strap—full of water. He lived in a dense jungle north of the village, in a hut of his own construction. He also carried iron tongs. For which god he served as priest, no one knew. Residing alone in the solitude of the jungle, his was an unconstrained, utterly fearless life. People knew him only as Jogi Baba, but his true name was Ramjit. People in the village assumed that he must be a worshipper of ghosts. Once a week he would come to our Dalit quarter of the village, where he would stand for a spell under a particular tree. His most extraordinary distinguishing quality was that whatever word a person in his presence uttered, he would instantaneously compose a three-line poem incorporating that word and sing it in his peculiar, rustic style. If someone were to utter the words "jogi baba," for example, he would immediately sing:

Jogi Baba sits in stillness
Patients seek relief from illness
Speak truthfully, Lord Ram
Speak truthfully, Lord Ram

Or if someone were to observe signs of an oncoming sandstorm—an aandhi—Jogi Baba would sing:

As the summer gives us aandhi
So was freedom brought by Gandhi
Speak truthfully, Lord Ram
Speak truthfully, Lord Ram

If the word "medicine" dropped from someone's lips, Jogi Baba would sing:

Medicine: the chemist makes it
Peace of mind: the family takes it
Speak truthfully, Lord Ram
Speak truthfully, Lord Ram

In this way Jogi Baba excelled in the art of spontaneous poetry. He had an astonishing capacity to redeploy any word—and this applied to thousands of words—instantly and in his inimitable style. Jogi Baba never spoke in prose. There has perhaps never been a soul quite like him in this world. Perhaps there never will be.

***

The month of Bhado holds an especially memorable place in my life. According to the Hindu religion Bhado is "kharvans," meaning a very inauspicious month. It so happened that in that same year of 1957, during the month of Bhado, the elderly mother of Sudessar, the Brahmin landlord for whom my father worked as ploughman, died. Amika Pandey—possessor of the magic almanac, discerner of auspicious times—happened to be one of Sudessar's tenants. Consulting his famous "patra," Amika Pandey declared that since the next fifteen days were inauspicious, the final rites of Sudessar's expired mother could not be performed. If the rites were conducted during this time, Sudessar's mother would suffer hell. Instead, Amika Pandey recommended that a grave be dug in the village death grounds and the mother's corpse be interred there for fifteen days, after which it could be exhumed and cremated according to Hindu final rites.

My father brought me with him to the death grounds to dig the grave. Father dug with a hoe, while I removed the soil. When the grave was ready, Sudessar Pandey, along with his tenants, brought the corpse to the grave and placed it inside. We then began to cover the corpse with earth, refilling the hole. First, though, as an amulet, Sudessar Pandey wrapped a golden ring in one corner of the burial shroud. According to local belief, if you tie gold into a burial shroud, the corpse will not decompose quickly. This was the advice of the Brahmins, and it was carried out. Father cut some sharp-thorned alangium bushes and placed them over the gravesite to deter wild animals. Having done all this, everyone returned home. In the following days Sudessar Pandey sent father to the death grounds to keep watch over the grave, as there was the constant threat that jackals would dig up the corpse and eat it. On several days, having his own work to do as well, father instructed me to go to the death grounds to keep watch in his place after I returned home from school for the day. I did as I was told, though I avoided the grave itself. I kept vigil from a slight distance. The death grounds were, in any case, not far from my route to school. Somehow in this way fifteen days passed, and the period of our grave-watching duties came to an end, as did the duration of inauspiciousness. Now came the time to exhume Sudessar's mother from the grave and cremate her corpse. During our fifteen-day vigil, my father often spoke of his worry that some thief, greedy for the gold ring, might dig up the body. It would be such an injustice. Father was so attached to his ploughman's bond that he was rather more concerned about the corpse of Sudessar Pandey's mother than Pandey was himself.

Finally, Amika Pandey, with his divine text, ascertained the appropriate time to disinter the body. Sudessar Pandey took four or five strokes with the hoe and then retreated to watch from a distance. Anticipating the stench, his tenants, too, fled from the spot. Father continued to remove earth with the hoe. To prevent the excavated dirt from sliding back into the grave, father had me shovel the soil further back from the edge. I did as I was told. Finally, within the grave, a glimpse of the shroud's white fabric came into view. All at once the odor of the decomposed corpse flooded the air. Suddesar Pandey pressed his scarf to his face and backed further away. From there he called out for father to first find the gold ring and take it out of the shroud. It was a strange moment. That day I learned that gold, for some, may be more precious than a mother's body.

Father told me to tie my scarf over my nose and mouth, and I did so. At that point all the Brahmins present made themselves scarce. Suddesar Pandey remained watching from a distance. Carefully, father managed to lift the two legs of the putrid corpse and place them in my hands. He then lifted the body from the head's side. Amid unutterable stench and nausea, the two of us lifted the corpse out of the ground and placed it upon a funeral pyre that had been arranged nearby. Extracting the gold ring from the shroud, father rubbed the ornament clean and returned it to Sudessar Pandey. With cloth tied over his nose and mouth, Pandey, with great difficulty, approached the pyre and set it aflame. He then retreated again to a distance. Next to the burning pyre, only father and I remained. When the blaze weakened, father broke off branches from a palash tree and added them to the pyre. The sun began to sink into the horizon. Slowly darkness spread. I began to feel afraid. Eventually the corpse was fully burned, and we picked up our hoes and came home. There was a little pond behind our home. In it we bathed and bathed. Father, after bathing, went to the peepul tree that he had planted when I was born. He lit clay lamps filled with ghee and prayed. He prayed in that same familiar manner, a kind of speaking while weeping, that I had heard all my life.

Who knows how many years those death grounds have incinerated people's sorrows, reducing them to ash. And who knows how many people's sufferings this place has entombed in its clay. And it will go on, burning and burying these afflictions. On that day I sensed that a death grounds had taken birth deep within me, a place in which unknowable sufferings would be buried or given the torch. When I finished high school and fled from home at the age of fifteen, I passed by those death grounds for the last time. I thought I was alone, yet in truth those death grounds journeyed with me. When I learned that this world is suffering, that there is a cause of this suffering, and that there is a means for its removal as well, it struck me that Gautam Buddha, before discovering these noble truths, must have at some point traveled through my village. The Tathagata must have walked by these very death grounds.

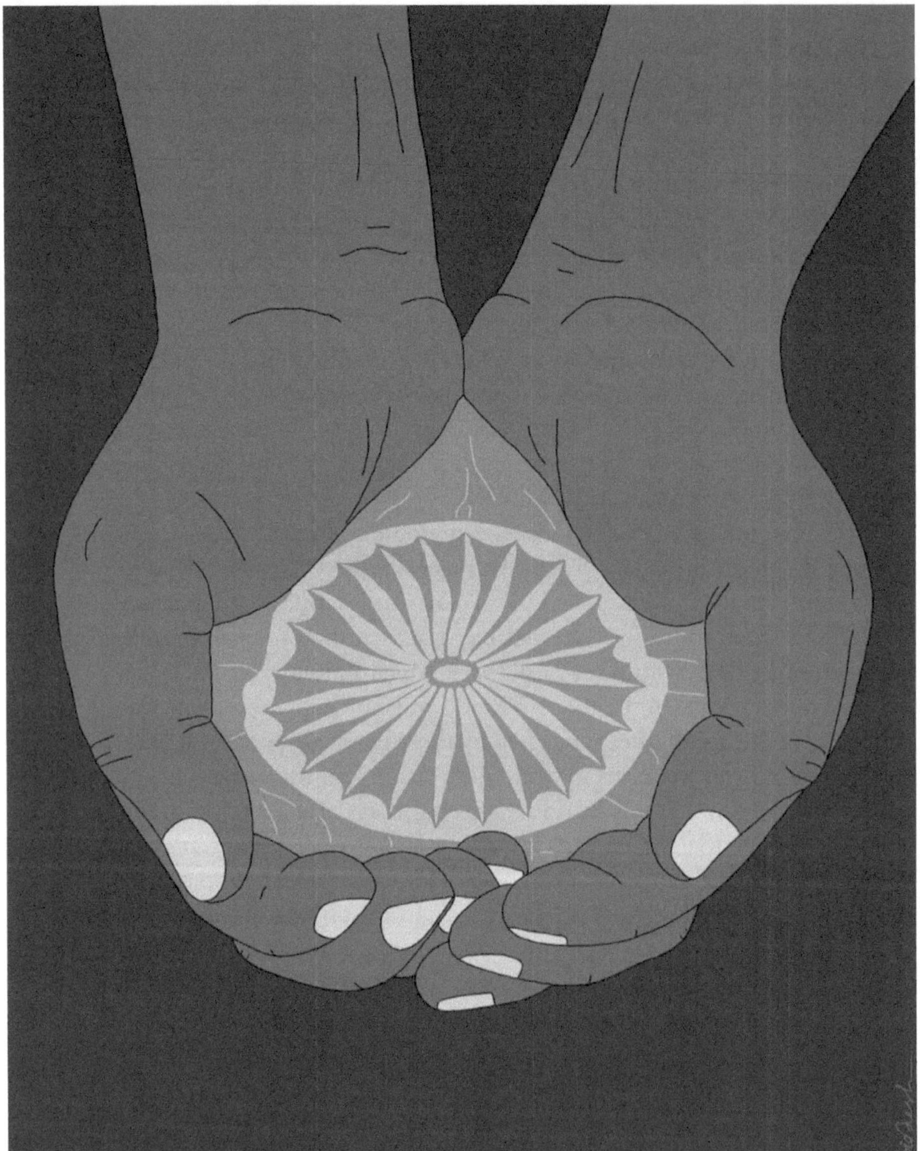

PRADNYA DAYA PAWAR

Searing through the Soul in Fatal Rhythm

A MARATHI POEM
TRANSLATED BY MAYA PANDIT

Translator's Note

Pradnya Daya Pawar is one of the most prolific writers in Marathi. She has published six poetry collections: Antastha *(Inside the Mind, 1993);* Utkat Jeevghenya Dhagiwar *(On Intense Killing Burning Heat, 2002);* Mi Bhidwu Pahatey Samagrashi Dola *(I Dare to Look in the Eye of the Whole, 2007);* Aarpar Layit Pranaatik *(Searing through the Soul in Fatal Rhythm, 2017);* Drushyancha Dhobal Samudra *(Sea of Obvious Scenes, 2013); and* Hillol Harwun Aatbahercha *(Tumult Within and Outside, 2024). And she has published one collection of short stories,* Afawa Khari Tharawi Mhanun *(So That the Rumors May Come True, 2010), along with three collections of her writings as a columnist, entitled* Kendra ani Parigh *(Center and Periphery, 2004);* Tehaltikori *(Observations from a Walk, 2015); and* Arwachin Aran *(Discourse Contemporary, 2020). She has written one play called* Dhadanta Khairlanji *(Blatantly, Khairlanji), and she has edited, along with Satish Kalsekar, a collection of selected poems by Namdev Dhasal entitled* Mi Bhayankarachya Darwajat Ubha Ahe *(I Stand at the Entrance of the Terrible, 2007).*

Pradnya took the literary world by storm with her poetry collections Antashtha *and* Utkat Jeevghenya Dhagiwar. *Fired by close encounters with the struggles of Dalit women, she internalized all the historical agony of the Dalit community, forced to live on the outskirts of the village, excommunicated, and suffering caste violence at various levels. Her amazing poetic idiom, her intense emotional reactions to the suffering of Dalit women in particular and women in general, and her indomitable rebellious spirit burst forth in fiery expressions of revolt. Her father, Daya Pawar, a wonderful poet who penned an explosive autobiography,* Baluta, *the first Dalit autobiography in India (1978), nurtured her creative urges at home. Pradnya has never looked back after the publication of her first poetry collections.*

When Pradnya began to write, the Dalit Literary Movement was charged with such stalwarts as Baburao Bagul, Namdev Dhasal, and Arjun Dangle.

There was a strong tradition developing of Dalit women's writing at that time. With writers like Baby Kamble, Sugandha Shende, Kausalya Baisantri, Meenakshi Moon, and Urmila Pawar and poets like Hira Bansode, Chaya Koregaonkar, Usha Ambhore, Sharada Navle, Jyoti Lanjewar, Hira Pawar, Shamal Garud, Pradnya had a strong tradition of Dalit women's writing to rely on. Yet she differs from them in many respects. Whereas most of these women wrote about their own experiences of how caste oppresses women, Pradnya goes beyond them in terms of her themes, ideological stance, and engagement with language.

Pradnya is very contemporary in her perception of women's condition in general, as she has been an active participant in the women's movement against caste violence, patriarchal controls, and state-sponsored violence. She has inherited the rebellious spirit from Dr. Ambedkar's philosophy, which has fused with insights from the intellectual energy of feminist struggles and writing. Dr. Ambedkar has explained how woman is the entrance of caste, as women's sexuality is controlled and exploited for keeping castes pure, and feminist perspectives have taught Pradnya to look at patriarchal machinations to keep women subjugated. That is why she explodes many myths about women in society, such as the sacredness of "motherhood" and of divisions among women between "monstrous" and "goddess-like" women represented by the mythical figures such as Hidimba, Tratika, and Putana, on the one hand, and Seeta, Savitri, and Urmila, on the other. In a sense she has subjected to critique the entire process of constructing women in popular imagination through religious and mythological means:

Hidimba, Tratika, Putana[1]
or Seeta, Savitri, Urmila[2]
nothing but the shadows
that carry on their heads
the container of myths
created by Powers that Be …
Pativratas,[3] *sinners, witches,*
adjectives replace common names …
… the grammatical suffixes and prefixes
move round and round, again and again

[1]Names of monster women in the Puranas. Hidimba was a monster who wanted to marry Bhima, one of the Pandavas. Tratika was a monster woman who would harass and attack sages performing yajñas in the forest. Putana was a monster who wanted to kill Baby Krishna with her poisonous milk. They are all enchantresses, with vile intentions.

[2]All three women are noted for their sacrifice for their husbands. Seeta accompanied Lord Rama to the forest; Savitri fought with Lord Yama, the God of Death, to get back her husband's life; and Urmila, the wife of Laxmana, Rama's brother, patiently waited for fourteen years for her husband to return from the forest.

[3]A pativrata is a devoted, faithful, and loyal wife who embodies marital fidelity and chastity and who is ready to sacrifice herself for her husband.

within the confines of the extremities of purity
Language reduced to a pulp
I can even tell you
When the signs changed their shapes![4]

She also exposed the casteist logic in the rapes that took place in the Dalit agitations:

Rapes happened
by an individual
or gang rapes
when the struggle for name change of the University intensified
she was paraded naked
so that Dalits could be taught a lesson
right in the middle of the street ...
she was raped brutally
in front of her daughters, daughters-in-law and sons-in-law
in Rajasthan ...
her genitals were slashed in Godhra ...[5]

The man–woman relationship and the concomitant inequality in traditional marriages has been one of the themes in her poetry right from the beginning. However, she is not trapped in the conventions of the typical women's language in writing of protest; there is no romanticism of the concept of love, and her poetry is distinctly away from loud outbursts of indignant outrage at women's oppression. In her very first collection, Pradnya declared rebelliously:

Manu awakened the ego in you
Who said women do not deserve freedom
And you also imprisoned yourself within the fence
The entire system was your witness!
But hark! This Cuckoo has shattered the shackles of that
disgrace
... And now she chooses to sing to her heart's content
Even in stark winter's frozen streams,
With open arms she welcomes the blue dreams
Though all alone for the time being.[6]

Pradnya confronts other areas of oppression as well. For instance, in 1872 the British Government declared many castes and communities as criminals by law. Separate settlements were created for them in which people from these communities were forced to live like animals. It was Pt Jawaharlal Nehru who demolished

[4]From *Mi Bhidwu Pahatey Samagrashi Dola*, 44–45.

[5]From *Mi Bhidwu Pahatey Samagrashi Dola*, 46–47.

[6]"Cuckoo," 1993, 4.

these settlements after India got freedom in the fifties. In the poem "Settlement" (1993), Pradnya seethes with rage at the ease with which entire communities were branded as criminals by birth and at their loss of their freedom.

Pradnya's feminist consciousness arises from her intense engagements with oppressive practices in traditional and postmodern ways of life. On the one hand, there are memories of the old oppressive world in which Dalits were forced to eat the flesh of dead animals. And on the other hand, in the modern world, there is a new world of commodities and fake desires created by global markets, which forces people to live in a particular way. This is also another form of slavery because there is no choice for people. The continuation of oppressive traditions in different forms creates a state of intense suffocation in her mind from which only a brand-new birth, she believes, will release her ("Brand new birth," 2002). She is very aware of the fractured nature of modernity in India, which carries the past and the present simultaneously. She vehemently rejects ideologies and practices that construct her in a way that is conducive to her oppression in the poem "Culture" and requests Culture as her mother to release her from the bonds of slavery.

Mother,
I don't want your holy black powder
nor your boundless heavy essence
nor the meaningless vacuum
of your extraordinary nothingness
You are power unlimited
the entrance of caste
the illusive liquid that spreads slowly
and captures my unspoken,
all the materiality of my being[7]

Pradnya's collection of poems, Sea of Obvious Scenes, *also marks her awareness of the condition of women in the world around her. She goes beyond the narrow confines of identity to sketch the travails of woman as a citizen of India and as a civic being, and delinks herself from formalist verbose outbursts of contemporary Dalit poetry to trace her roots to the* Therigatha, *the poetry of the Buddhist nuns of centuries ago. She rebels against the established oppressive language that prohibits communication and crosses over the so-called profound meanings determined by the Centre to reach out to the Periphery to understand the communications of the dispossessed ("Communication," 2013). The poems in this collection are marked by an affinity to the natural disposition and inherent constitution of "human beings" as "humane" beings. One major feature of the poems in this collection is the almost total absence of loud slogan-like expressions. Instead, there is an exploration of the inner recesses of consciousness from*

[7]2002, 63.

where several spirals of agony spring forth with their amazing power to reveal the mechanisms of suffering. In her poem "Written, Not Written ...," she declares that when everything that she had created from the threads of her being, like simple dreams, freshness of innocent laughter, and intense involvement—that is, everything that she had earned with her tears and blood—was completely destroyed, she set forth upon a new journey:

Thus with these bags of darkness
on my back
I set forth a long time back
on this journey
to break open the layers
of new possibilities
with my transient intellect[8]

These poems represent her intense involvement with language.

With her last collection of poems, Hillol Harwun Aat-Bahercha *(1924), Pradnya seems to have entered a stage of introspective philosophical musings. She seems to explore the meanings of being human in an atmosphere marked by stark, naked violence and terror. Rohit Vemula, and Bilkis Banu and Ayesha Sheikh, women horribly treated by fanatical ultraright men, form the pivot of her representation of reality. She argues that public and private seem to have merged in the darkness that unfolds us and compares our life to Guernica, Picasso's famous painting. In such an atmosphere, she says:*

I hold tightly to the branch of poetry
the only branch left for support
just like a young Dombari girl
walks on a taut and swaying string
I do my tight rope walk
maintaining balance
putting my life as stakes[9]

Pradnya has published short stories that portray the consciousness of educated Buddhist women in the changing scenario of the metropolitan spaces. Collected in Afwa Khari Tharawi Mhanun *(2010), translated by me into* Let the Rumours Be True *(2018), these stories deal with the issues of intercaste marriage, of being de-casted, of the psychology of upper-caste women in jobs previously done by lower-caste women, and of women who have freed themselves from the burden of past traditions, which seem to have a tremendous hold on their husbands. These stories explore the hitherto unexplored areas of the psychological distances women have traveled with their Buddhist consciousness and*

[8]"Written, Not Written," 2013, 78.

[9]*Hillol Harwun Aatbahercha*, 1924, 99.

how a more enlightened woman explores the meaning of her existence in a world of new technological advances such as the internet and social media platforms, where her sexuality is again exploited through deception, trickery, and fraud.

Dhadanta Khairlanji *is a play Pradnya has written based on the gruesome Khairlanji incident, where an entire village rose against a Dalit family to gang rape the women and massacre the entire family of four. Pradnya's play does not deal with this incident directly but rather talks about the discourse of falsification that intellectuals, media, and cinema people indulge in. The play demonstrates how the so-called radical intellectuals and media people try to falsify history and change a gruesome story completely to gain viewership and profits. Pradnya exposes the deadly logic of the entertainment industry, which is far removed from either idealism or social vision and for which every violent political incident is looked upon as a gold mine to mint money through gross misrepresentation of reality.*

Pradnya also has published her prose writing in the form of three books, two of which, Kendra Ani Parigh *and* Tehaltikori, *are collections of her columns. The most important book among her prose writings is* Arwachin Aaran *(The Modern Battleground, 2020), where she discusses several contemporary issues in today's India and Maharashtra; the book also contains some major long poems on the contemporary scene.*

Pradnya worked as an associate professor and head of the Department of Marathi at Satish Pradhan Dyanasadhana College in Thane, Maharashtra, till 2023, when she took voluntary retirement on account of health issues. This Marathi poet, columnist, and writer has been awarded a number of prestigious awards at the state as well as national levels:

- *Maharashtra Foundation, 2009 (USA)*
- *Birsa Munda Sanman Puraskar by Ramnika Foundation, Ranchi, Jharkhand, in 2009*
- *Bodhivardhan Puraskar by Babasaheb Ambedkar Shatakmanotsav Committee Trust, Sphurtidham, Bangalore in 2010*
- *Gangadhar Gadgil Puraskar by Popular Prakashan, Mumbai 2022*
- *Attendance at the World Book Fair in Moscow, Russia, as part of the NBT (National Book Trust) authors delegation in September 2009*
- *The Maharashtra State Government Award in 2015 (which she returned in protest against the rising intolerance in the country)*

Many of her books and poems have also been published in translation:

Let the Rumours Be True *(a collection of short stories). Translated into English by Maya Pandit (2017), AuthorsUpFront Publishing Services.*

Pradnya Daya Pawar Kathegalu *(a collection of short stories). Translated into Kannada by Chandrakant Pokale (2012), Kanva Prakashan, Bangalore.*

Select poems have been translated into Urdu and published in Dalit Awaz, *ed. Yakub Rahi (1998), Adshot Publications, Mumbai.*

Select poems have been published in an anthology of Marathi Poetry titled Navya Wata, Navi Walne, *ed. Nishikant Mirajkar, 2008, published by Penguin India, New Delhi.*

Select poems have been published in an anthology of Marathi Poetry titled Drushyantar, *ed. Chandrakant Patil, 2007, published by National Book Trust, New Delhi.*

Translations of her Poems have been published in various journals in Urdu, Kannada, Gujarati, Hindi, Pahadi, Malayalam, Tamil, English, Italian, and Russian as well as English, for example in Indian Literature, Samakalin Bharatiya Sahitya, Hansa, Antarang Sangini, Anyatha, *and* Yuddharat Aam Aadmi.

List of Pradnya Daya Pawar's publications:
Poetry Collections:

Antastha *(Inside the Mind) (1993) 1st Ed., Mansanman Prakashan, Pune, 2nd Ed. (2004), Dimple Publication, Mumbai.*

Utkat Jivghenya Dhagiwar *(On Intense Burning Heat) (2002), Lokwangmay Griha, Mumbai.*

Mi Bhidavu Pahatey Samagrashi Dola *(I Dare to Look in the Eye of the Whole) (2007), Granthali Publication, Mumbai.*

Aarpar Layit Pranatik *(Soul Searing Fatal Rhythm) (2009) 1st Ed., (2010), 2nd Ed. (2017), 3rd Ed., Lokwangmay Griha, Mumbai.*

Drushyancha Dhobal Samudra *(The Sea Obvious Scenes) (2013), Popular Prakashan, Mumbai.*

Hillol Harwun Aat-Bachercha *(Tumult Within and Outside) (2024), Popular Prakashan, Mumbai.*

Mi Bhayankarachya Darwajat Ubha Ahe *(I Stand at the Entrance of the Terrible) – A collection of Selected Poems of Mamdeo Dhasal (2007), Shabda Publication, Mumbai, Edited along with Satish Kalsekar.*

Play:

Dhadant Khairlanji *(Blantantly, Khairlanji), A Two-Act Play (2007), Pratishabda Prakashan, Mumbai.*

Short Stories:

Afwa Khari Tharavi Mhanun *(So That Rumours Come True), A Collection of Short Stories (2010), Shabda Publications, Mumbai.*

Prose Collections:

Kendra Ani Parigh *(Centre and Periphery), A Collection of Column Writings (2004), Dimple Publication, Mumbai.*

Tehaltikori *(Observations of a Wanderer), A Collection of Column Writings (2015), Akshar Prakashan, Mumbai.*

Arwachin Aaran *(Modern Battleground), A Collection of Column Writings, speeches etc (2020), Shabda Publications, Mumbai.*

Vimuktanche Swatantrya *(Freedom of the Nomadic Tribes) Edited along with Narayan Bhosale and Vinayak Lashkar (2018), Pariwartanacha Watsaru Prakashan, Thane.*

Context for the Poem:

This translation of a long Marathi poem entitled *Aarpaar Layit Pranantik* is addressed to Vithabai Bhau Mang Narayangaonkar, a legendary Tamasha artist in Maharashtra famous for her melodious lavanis and beautiful dancing.

Vithabai was born in a Mang family in 1935 in Pandharpur in Solapur district, Maharashtra, India. She was the fourteenth and last child of her parents. She grew up in a family of artists. Her father, Bhau-Bapu Mang Narayangaonkar, ran a family troupe, and she imbibed the tamasha culture from childhood and performed with amazing splendor on stage right from a very young age, without any formal training in either acting, music, or dance. Yet, she had to struggle with poverty all through her life. A man called Maruti Vishnu Sawant, captivated by her beauty, married Vithabai, and she gave birth to eight children from him. Sawant deceived her, financially exploited her, and abandoned her. After he left, she ran her troupe with more than one hundred and fifty artistes and took care of them. Yet she remained loyal to Sawant. When he was on his deathbed, she came back and nursed him till the end.

Vithabai was called the "Tamasha Samradini" (Tamasha Empress) and won high accolades from people. She was honored with the prestigious President's Award in the Tamasha genre of art (1957 and 1990) and was awarded the Sangeet Natak Akademi Award, a national award in India, as well as "Maharashtra Gaurav Puraskar" of the Maharashtra Government. The Government of Maharashtra instituted an annual "Vithabai Narayangaonkar Lifetime Achievement Award" in her memory in 2006. Vithabai was the President of the Dalit Natya Sammelana, in which she spoke forthrightly about the issues and problems of Tamasha artists. She also went to the NEFA border region in 1962 to entertain Indian soldiers fighting on the China front.

One of the notable events of Vithabai's life involved her performing on stage while nine months pregnant. She came to know during the performance that she was about to deliver. She went backstage, delivered the baby, cut the umbilical cord with a stone, and came back to join the performance.

Toward the end of her life, Vithabai became quite destitute. She survived on the meager amount she was paid in a Tamasha troupe on a nightly basis. She had no money even for her medical treatment, and her last rites were performed with donations collected from friends and well-wishers.

Nobody is free here
and especially you
you were born with suffering
tied to your ankle bells from birth
for nine months and nine days

you had carried both in that sack of skin
along with the blazing musical notes in your heart
and lightning sparks in your feet

"Face like a beautiful fairy
two stunning knolls below the neck
eyes like piercing knives
how you wound the poor hearts"[10]

Vithabai
this tragedy, is not just yours alone
Writing is for the Brahmans
farming is for the Kunbis[11]
and singing flows in the blood
of our community

You bowed down your head
to the shadow of traditional wisdom
a shadow cast without any light
you knotted the maya[12] of hierarchy in your pallu ...

Gan, gaulan, wag, lavani, batawani, rangabaji ...[13]
a riot of art of diverse parts
but how many times in the darkness of the tent,
did you swallow the surging seas of suffering within?
Duff, kanda, dholki, sambal, tuntuna ...[14]
the instruments played your lifc
and with the same lifelong loyalty
you owed to the black beads around your neck,
the same loyalty

---

[10]Literal translation of the way a woman's beauty used to be described in traditional "Lavani," that is, erotic songs, in the Tamasha, a folk art of Maharashtra.

[11]Kunbi is supposed to be a subcaste of the Maratha Caste, who have traditionally been farmers.

[12]"Maya" means illusion in the traditional Hindu, Brahmanical philosophy. All reality is considered to be "Maya," an illusion that prohibits true spiritual knowledge.

[13]These are parts of Tamasha. Tamasha begins with a "Gan," which is a song of Krishna, followed by "Gaulan," the song and dance of the milkmaids of Mathura whom Krishna and his friend Pendya tease. This is followed by "Wag," based on a Puranic or folk tale. Lavani is an erotic song accompanied by dance. "Batawani" usually means cheating, but here it is comic dialogue between characters. "Rangbaji" involves songs and dances by a group of artistes who entertain the audiences with their humorous and occasionally vulgar dialogues.

[14]"Duff" is a kind of small flat drum; "Dholki" is a big drum played from both sides. It can be hung around the neck. A "Sambal" is a drum made of brass, wood, parchment, iron, and cotton that contributes to the music in a big way. "Tuntuna" is a single-string instrument. All of these musical instruments are used in other folk art forms as well.

you showed to your act,
your performance,
your dance,
the same loyalty—
to the purest form of your art
to unadulterated passions
glances and embraces
as part of your act
that captivated a million hearts
You devastated
the anthills and hillocks
strangleholds of classical dictates
The fragrance of your raw soil
spread everywhere
intense and intoxicating.

Vithabai,
I know you are exhausted,
your body is old and wrinkled
but please make an entry
once again
on the Tamasha Stage
and let that Kalgi Tura[15]
take place once for all
for the last time.
Ask the silver coin of a rupee[16]
"What does the coin desire?"

Sing at least once
the melody of your wretched life,
of the flowing clotting blood,
of your bonds with grief
melodies of your suffering
songs of your aches and agony
of the dreadful misery
of your own birth n' death …

[15]Kalgi-Tura is a Marathi folk art form, a predecessor to the well-known Tamasha, characterized by the use of spiritual ballad poetry. This is a poetic philosophical dialogue between followers of Goddess Shakti (Kalgi) and God Shiva (Tura) about who is superior.

[16]A rupee coin would be flung on the stage at the dancer by a prestigious spectator to ask her to sing and dance to a particular song, and she would ask this question.

O Lady Mother, O my Holy Ma
bring once again
your spirited act alive
which began with the story of woman
and ended with the same woman
the story of Vithabai Bhau Mang Narayangaokareen.

This bit part has no end
Why would you even take stock
of the intense desire for Love
suffering was born
and kept dying afresh
again and again
yet you enjoyed
the intoxicating magical bliss of flesh

Apart from your moaning uterus
believe me, seriously,
you had plenty of other stuff immemorial
You whipped up a powerful storm
with abandon
of vibrant passion,
sharp nails honed to an edge
eyes penetrating the spectators' hearts
stirring a desire sharp as a needle,
famished, you kept on consuming
the pure unadulterated thirst
that'd scorched your throat
from Time immemorial.

They didn't allow you to remain
simple and easy as the earth
slowly you got transformed into
a material object
to be owned and bonded
the so-called civilized culture
tore you apart
from your own natural Self.

You had to stand
with the heavy ankle bells binding your feet
amid the thick dung heaps
of masculine hounding
you too danced a ferocious dance,

as an enchanted thunder enhanced
the representation of the Primordial Form
of illusion and beauty!
You were put in a cage
though you never looked like
a slave beauty with sex appeal,
but burned with a helpless rage.

You kept on singing
the song of the biological quagmire
where all men and women are born
A song that was
intense and vigorous
free as a lark
Your laughter was always
clean, innocent, unrestrained,
you became more n' more natural
and climbed down easily
so many frivolous, fake levels of
pretentious Truth
to gracefully glide to the bottom
only to see clearly
what exactly it was that lay hidden
under the honor of the red bindi[17]
worn by the married woman:
a sign of status, dignity and respect!
You exposed the truth at last!

Who is on this side
of the liberation line
dark yet scintillatingly bright
and who can be said
to be just beyond?

The life story of Caste, Class and Woman's Life
is not something that one
sails through with a careless glance
A story
not just a coincidence
of a biological accident
The society is constructed
along a scale of

[17]Bindi is the red tikka on the forehead of a woman, considered to be sacred.

innate inequality,
infinite and boundless!

And woman
flares like a flag
her whole life
loyal to the boundaries drawn!

At the foothold are buried
all historical evidences
that differentiate
the vagina from the petals of flowers
right from the Khyber Pass[18]
to the Anklets and Tuntune

Your hardy and resilient journey
was not really futile and worthless
You did free the language
from the stranglehold of male domination
brought it out in its naked form
You took the poisonous cobra sting[19]
on the tip of your tongue,
an open challenge!
and you were transformed
into a myth
the same process
from Pavala Hivargaonkar to[20]
Vithabai Bhau Mang Narayangaonkar

What difference does it make really?
there's just the face of a woman
What difference does the name make?
or even the face, for that matter?
It can be "Pavala"
or it can be "Vithabai"
What difference does it make?

---

[18]The Khyber Pass is a mountain pass in the Khyber Pakhtunkhwa province of Pakistan, on the border with the Nangarhar Province of Afghanistan. In Indian history, this pass has played an important role, as most of the tribes from Iran, Afghanistan, and other countries migrated to India through this pass.

[19]Cobra Sting: It was a belief that magicians who did black magic would get a cobra to sting their tongue.

[20]Pavala Hivargaonkar was another famous Tamasha artist in 1885. The Maharashtra Government Award for Tamasha Artists is named after her.

whether a woman comes from
Mahar, Mang, Dhor, Chambhar caste?[21]
Or Kolhati
Or Dombari?

You stood firm
even within this rigmarole
of sex and caste
woven so tight
Your feet firmly planted
on the soil
of your locality on the margins
that was your base
You stood firm, unshaken!
in the narrow confines of that space!

The small pit of appetite
the drum of dearth
the eternal story of hunger
the batawani of pollution
to the tune
of millions of sawal-jawabs[22]
dances Pavala to that refrain
dances Vitha to the same refrain.

Body as the weapon
Yet going beyond the body
Celebrating the body
With the body as the means!

"Eika Dajiba"[23]
"Listen O Dajiba"

---

[21]These are the names of the lowest of the low castes in the caste hierarchy. In general, women and men from these castes worked in the Tamasha, the greatest and most popular entertainment among folk arts. The Mahar people were also utilized as messengers or village guards. The Mang community prepared ropes from a particular grass called "Ghaypat" for farmers. The Chambhar caste made shoes from leather. The Kolhati community was a nomadic community that played acrobatics in the streets for survival. The Dombari community also played in the streets and presented their acrobatic skills for survival. Many drummers in Tamasha came from this caste.

[22]In the Tamasha, there used to be a series of questions ("sawal") and answers ("jawab") between two groups in a competition. These would be often impromptu and would be based on folk beliefs and stories of Puranic origin. They would be like riddles.

[23]Dajiba is a term of respect in the rural areas. A Tamasha artist would address the male spectators by this name.

See this eternal play
of a woman's body
with the dhol and the stick[24]
See the play
till your eyes pop out;
but don't forget
witness here
my Eternal Man;
with a black, sturdy,
pole-straight body
eternally standing firm
his feet rooted
for ages in the soil
beating the dhol.
He is my original MAN
see him along with
his poverty, suffering
and the travails he has faced
He has understood the strife,
the millions of contradictions
implicit in different layers of life.

How my soul shatters in a million pieces!
He is the one
who's cuddled each fiber of my being
my glances, my performances
my acts and my facts
He saw my pains and aches
my toil and my labor
as an organic part of me
never as an appendage
outside of me.
For him
they were all embodied parts of mine
indivisible, enduring,
everlasting through time.
Only he knew
how the flame dances
Only he could smell
the fresh breeze blowing
its magical charm
in the space outside

[24]Dhol is a big drum played with two sticks.

the woman's bodily form
and her skin's glamour
steeped in allure!
all the agony, warm, salty
spread over my sharp pupils
mutely flowing down my eyes
he would absorb with the tip of his tongue
the agony of being a human being
that was like seawater
a warm, saline, melted life.

What is this dialectic
in the historical evolution
that neither allows a man to be primordial
nor even to be the man
that can be ultimate and final!

The inner themes
of the philosophy
are nothing but clotted blood

Your past
tears away at me
it's oh! So cruel!

My past, too,
tears away at me
it's oh! So cruel!

The past of all of us
all women together
tears away at me
it's oh! So cruel!
When will come to light
our millions of stories
like a river that suddenly
vanishes underground to flow
to surface one day
in a dancing bouncing spring

They have arrested
our present life
captured it
but it's still alive

This neo-capitalism,
this huge grinding stone,
operates without any remote control,
your intense original hues
and the vibrant statements of the ostracized
all thrashed black and blue
it ultimately grinds them to fine dust.

In cutthroat competition
the new fake Lavani
is being marketed
"Listen O Dajiba, listen to me
A scorpion has bitten me"[25]
they whitewash
the image of the Empress of Lavani
to project it with fake sheen
on the monstrous global screen
It's humiliation, pure and simple!
the Tamasha artists
the same humiliation
the Bahujan face[26]
the same humiliation
the womanhood faces
the same humiliation.

A woman is nothing but
a container of sexualized flesh
wicked wanton flesh
licentious, lustful flesh
that titillates
allures
mesmerizes
and causes her fall
and the downfall of all of us.

Will there be any true son of a mother?
honorable, noble, decent
who will be able to read and save

---

[25]These lines are quoted from a traditional popular lavani.

[26]Bahujan is a term used for people from all the non-Brahman castes. According to Mahatma Phule's polemics, the society was divided into two castes: Brahmans and non-Brahmans. The term "Bahujan" (majority of all non-Brahman people, Kashtriya + Vaishya + Shudra + Ati-Shudras, i.e., Dalits) was actually used later by Vitthal Ramji Shinde to describe all the non-Brahman castes. So, a Baniya also would be a Bahujan in this discourse.

the damp dark space
in your primordial uterus?

As the pages of the calendar fly,
entire localities on the margins
are being transformed into malls
Patriarchy, caste and class
The same old skeletons
have developed new cells
and broken out into monstrous blossoms
that flourish like hell.

How long shall I send messages
How long shall I be the conscience keeper
How long shall I take care of the watan lands?[27]
How long shall I ruthlessly prune myself
and swear by my honesty?
How long shall I sing my suffering
in the gorgeous palace of my grandeur?
How long shall I hang my eternal grief
onto the sparkling chandelier?

Massacred
sexually looted
regularly, brutally
in broad daylight
my mothers and sisters

Sugar Lobby
Cooperatives
Milk Producers' Companies
Zillah Parishads[28]
Spinning Mills
MIDC
Corporations
Taluka Panchayats,[29] Market Committees
forcing women to dance
to do Daulatjada[30]

---

[27]Lands given to the Mahar and other lower castes by feudal kings and landlords.

[28]Local self-governing bodies at the district level in India's Panchayat Raj system.

[29]These are local self-governing bodies in the Panchayat Raj system at the Taluka (Block) level.

[30]A custom in the Tamasha where the woman artist had to sit in the lap of the landlord or rich man for his sexual gratification.

The strangleholds of
the castles of Power and Pelf
can't be breached

With the deepening night
darkness sparkles bright
in the naked empire
of sovereign state
Identities are broken bit by bit
the six vikaras[31] are celebrated
with shameless greed
the Tamasha women always bear
the unwanted seed.

A giant octopus
called poverty
takes birth again and again
with the Kavachkundalas[32]
of the dispossessed.

Thousands of tiny hands
keep looking for food
along with dogs and cats
keep looking for legitimate friends
for their mothers around
in the insufferable mix
of murky slime that abounds.

The protesting sun
rises every day in vain
takes to his heels silently
from a narrow side lane
to save himself the shame.

We are the prostitutes
of Lord Indra's court ...

---

[31]Vikaras: These are the six disorders or vices according to Indian philosophy. These are Lobha (Avarice), Krodh (Anger), Mada (Arrogance), Moha (Temptations), Matsar (Envy), and Kama (Sexual Desire). They are also known as Shadripu, that is, six enemies of man.

[32]Kavachkundala: Divine protection gifted to a person in the form of some body element that makes the person invincible. (Karna in the Mahabharata, e.g., was gifted with divine earrings.) Here the lower birth is referred to ironically as a gift from God, as He keeps an account of one's sins and merits in this life and decides which caste one will be born into in the next life. All women and all Bahujan are "Papayonis," as they are sinners by default.

We are the prostitutes
of Lord Indra's court ...
The song rises
higher and higher
in the air-conditioned camp
of the high fliers

Vithamai, my mother
I cannot look at you
as an antique piece
in some museum,
nor as a package
of cultural heritage
saved for future generations.
nor can I look at you
as a woman in the service of the nation
in the camp on the NEFA border[33]
to entertain the soldiers.

I cannot, just cannot, display
only a little objectivity
only a little curiosity
Only a little unease
only a little empathy
only a little sensitivity
for your wretched life

I know, O my Mother,
the fires of suffering
that a woman seeks to douse
by pouring liquor down her throat
I know
the blank space called woman
the woman who has forgotten
the password of her identity

Vithamai
that Maruti Sawant[34]
snatched away your passbook

---

[33]Vithabai had gone to the NEFA border region to entertain the Indian soldiers fighting in the China war in 1962.

[34]Maruti Sawant was the husband of Vithabai, who exploited her and then left her. But she took care of him when he was in the last stage of his life.

That Maruti Sawant
snatched away your swaying figure
That Maruti Sawant
snatched away
your unique humanness un-breached
That Maruti Sawant
gave his name
as a legitimate father
to your little ones
That Maruti Sawant
snatched you away
from your own being!
Maruti Sawant
from Narayangaon
from Pune
from Maharashtra
from India.

No Vithabai is able to play
the game of hitting below the belt
after exploiting him to the hilt
as they say
Naturally
you had inherited
the stranglehold of tradition
so when Maruti Sawant
began his death rattle
and wanted to see you
you forgave him all his sins
and fulfilled his last wish
with heartfelt compassion
When he was placed on the funeral pyre
you wiped the kumkum off your forehead.[35]
You'd put it there in his name all your life.
with faith, loyalty and devotion
You carried his widowhood on your shoulders
to walk on the "noble" track of tradition!

My eyes swell
my throat chokes dry

---

[35]Kumkum is a red powder, like a bindi, a mark of a married woman, which is considered sacred. The tradition is to wipe off the kumkum from a widow's forehead when her dead husband is placed on the funeral pyre.

something is stuck there
What chemical were you born with, Mother?
The sweat flowing
down your neck, armpits, cleavage
down your back, thighs
the sweat flowing all through
the sweat in the darkness of your anklets
Finally, it gathered and stopped
near the intense melody of your song.
The sweat was there
when you danced with
a nine-month pregnancy
and when while dancing
there was a gut-wrenching pain
you went quietly to the backstage
gave birth to your baby
cut off the placenta with a stone
then returned to the stage
to resume the erotic dance of Rangabaji
the sweat then dripped through
your vagina, your thighs, your legs
the sweat!
O, the rivulets of sweat!

The agony sears through my heart
my senses
and you sing
With a graceful round
"I choose you my love, O my heart's desire
Don't abandon this palace of pleasure"

Vithamai, Mother
all the honors conferred on you
from the President's Medal to Sangeet Natak Akademi Award
you have become a myth
much discussed, much talked about
in the seminar culture
All those documentaries
those films on you;
these so-called intucs[36]
bookish men in the Universities
scratch their pedantic heads, and

---

[36]A derogatory form of "intellectuals."

scribble some obscure stuff on
"The Female Principle in Folk Arts"
Blah … blah … blah … blah …
Lavani festivals are organized
to salute you.
and challenge one with the remark
There is a poem in the picture!
while you
destitute, famished, starving
beg in the name of the goddess
with a bowl in your hand!

How long
will this play of primordial hunger
go on
How long will your bugdi[37]
go on getting lost, like this?
How long will you pace around
in and out of the space of your body?
searing the soul in gut-wrenching rhythm
How long?
How long will you sing,
the glorified song of deception?
of destitution?
of deprivation?
This song which was yours once
this same song has become mine today
the song of unwavering, unshaken
of pure unadulterated passion!
how do I stop this song?
Shall I sing it like you, unbeaten
this serene and primordial song?
in the same way as you sing
aloud, charged with efficacy?
yet overflowing with fragile delicacy?

Who stole my voice
I can't even be a zilkari[38]
shall I dance wildly
madly, passionately?

---

[37]An earring.

[38]Zilkaris are the accompanists standing in a group behind the main singer in Tamasha. They provide him/her with repetitions of the refrain, or chorus.

in the ugly limelight of the hundred percent agenda
of foul and obnoxious global schema?

Come on, come on,
someone, get up
tie to my feet
the huge anklets with tinkling beads

Let me write too
brand new pages of history
What is the nature
of materiality of travails
How it crosses over
the hunger in your body and soul
How it churns out
the entire life upside down

Let me too write about
a passionate, ardent and scintillating account
in the name of Woman
in the name of a Dalit Woman
in the name of a Black Woman
in the name of the Tamasgir Woman[39]
in the name of Pavala
in the name of Vithabai![40]

---

[39]Tamasgir is one who performs in the Tamasha.

[40](Translation of the long poem *Aarpaar Layit Pranantik* ... [Mumbai: Lokawangmaya Gruha, 2009 1st ed., 2010 2nd ed., and 2017 3rd ed.].)

Literary Navigations: Focus on the Craft and Practice of International Writing and Publishing

Grounded in *Mānoa's* identity as a journal of international writing, with a special interest in the Pacific, Asia, and the Americas, LITERARY NAVIGATIONS is a section devoted to exploring the craft and practice of literary creation and presentation in a global context of reading. Brief essays (2000–2500 words) examine challenges as well as opportunities in the practice of the literary when crossing boundaries of all kinds and at all levels from the word to the book. The section presents spirited reflections by writers, editors, and translators on the practice and presentation of writing between languages, audiences, cultures, nations, histories, and more.

S. SHANKAR

On Literary Greatness and Endangered Literary Cultures

When considering literary matters in a global context, monoculturalism is to be resisted. "Literature" is at once a very narrow and a very broad signifier, depending on who is using the term and how. At its narrowest—that is, its most monocultural—"literature" can mean "great writing" according to some (presumably) clearly delineated criteria of global relevance. At the other end of the spectrum, at its broadest, "literature" signifies traditions of the word manifesting imaginative labor—*word* rather than *writing* because, at this broadest of levels, literature has made, as it should, space for the oral. At this end of the spectrum, traditions of the word are of great diversity, and they don't all agree on how "greatness" is to be understood. To my mind, the latter approach to "literature" is generally more defensible. Which is why, rather than the common idea of World Literature, I generally find more useful the notion of "literatures of the world," where the plural recognizes multiple and sometimes contradictory conceptions of literary value.

Literary value in World Literature would seem to be straightforward—World Literature is great literature, recognizable as such across the world. Covered up in this thought is the reality that "World Literature" is generally understood as per aesthetic principles perfected historically within European and Western literary contexts. In contrast, the conundrum of literary value within a "literatures of the world" context, that is, a context of multiple word traditions with multiple ideas of greatness, is much more difficult, though here difficulty is not something to be feared.

What I am getting at might be illustrated by reference to Tamil ideas of literary greatness. These Tamil ideas are often intimately connected to language, that is, the greatness of the Tamil language in itself. Here "the greatness conception," if one might call it that, is that Tamil is a uniquely beautiful language and in great Tamil works that beauty shines through clearly. This conception admits the possibility of individual genius but regards such genius as oriented to the revelation of the unique beauty of Tamil. A conundrum follows: how can texts produced, consumed, celebrated, and canonized under such criteria ever travel outside of Tamil through translation? Simply put, how could a Tamil text regarded as great according to these criteria, which are linked so closely to a particular manifested language, be recognized as great in any other language? Because of the difficulties posed by such questions, I believe we should pluralize our ideas of aesthetics and greatness in addition to our ideas of literature(s).

To be clear, not all ideas of greatness in Tamil are language-based. Other ideas of "greatness" exist within Tamil literary—that is, word—traditions. Tamil, like other languages, has imported many literary notions from across the world, most substantially from Europe because of British colonial influence. These importations have only increased over time, and so, now, very many ideas of literary value are shared between Tamil and Europe (and other parts of the world). At the same time, indigenous contrary notions of literary value, some going back millennia, continue to be espoused and circulate within the Tamil literary sphere. In acknowledging the conundrum of greatness within a plural "literatures of the world" context, there is no need to insist on complete difference between Tamil and all other literary spheres. It is enough simply to remind ourselves that differences exist and should be recognized.

The conundrum of discussing literature in a global context is compounded by the fact that literary activities outside of the global metropoles of culture (mainly Europe and North America) are especially hard to recognize and acknowledge. Partly, this is because aesthetic principles are crafted and exported from the metropole much more robustly than from the periphery. Another reason is that the sheer volume of visible literary activity—and activity visible as literary—is much greater in the metropole than in the periphery. Even with the best of intentions, it is hard to practice attentiveness to peripheral literary productions given the unavailability of materials (e.g., translations) as well as the absence of the requisite knowledge (of languages, cultures, and aesthetic principles).

These observations on the literary productions of metropole and periphery are fairly obvious. Holding fast to the idea that literary value ("greatness," if you like) is quite separate from metropolitan or peripheral status is harder. Many literary productions are deserving of serious attention despite their peripheral origin, and sometimes even because of it, for it is possible to argue that great peripheral literary texts push the boundaries of the literary in ways that metropolitan texts do not. They challenge metropolitan aesthetic principles and de-normalize them. Often, they manifest alternative ideas of literary value against great odds, enacting spectacular imaginative feats.

Because the ideas I am exploring are of universal scope, I will mention two writers, widely separated geographically, whose work I know well and who I think deserve serious consideration when it comes to recognizing literary value in a global context: Ngũgĩ wa Thiong'o and Albert Wendt. The careers of both these writers, in different ways, challenge metropole-based ideas of literary value.

Ngũgĩ wa Thiong'o was an African writer perhaps unrivaled in his influence because he was not only a novelist and dramatist but also a widely read critic. His literary achievement has range and depth. Novels like *A Grain of Wheat* (1967), *Petals of Blood* (1977), *Matigari* (1986, trans. from Gikuyu into English by Wangũi wa Goro), and *Wizard of the Crow* (trans. from Gikuyu into English by the author, 2007) are ambitious and innovative, pushing at the boundaries of novelistic form. From certain conventional standards they may be found wanting, but I would argue that rather than "lack," Ngũgĩ's novels manifest a bending of the form of the novel that reflects the influence of peripheral aesthetics. Ngũgĩ has often argued the importance of orature in relation to literature. Famously, he has fashioned himself a writer in two languages (English and Gikuyu). Both Ngũgĩ's mining of oral traditions and his insistence on pursuing a literary career in both English and Gikuyu represent a challenge to extant monocultural norms of literary greatness. Ngũgĩ has not only embodied the challenge to literary monoculture in literary works—drama and life writing in addition to fiction—but also in criticism. Works like *Decolonizing the Mind* (1986) and *Globalectics* (2012) have left indelible marks on critical conversation today.

In a different way, Albert Wendt, the towering figure of Pacific (or Oceania) literature, too poses a challenge to normative, global literary monoculture. Wendt is a Samoan writer based in New Zealand. His main reputation is as a novelist, and the work of his I know best is *Leaves of the Banyan Tree* (1979), an epic novel that touches on themes of colonialism and social change in the South Pacific. *Leaves* is also a masterful work of great formal scope; different parts of the novel present different modes of narrative; and the novel as a whole integrates Indigenous storytelling as well as psychological realism. Wendt is a powerful Indigenous writer, that is, a writer who identifies with living traditions of the Pacific extending to before European contact. Wendt draws on these Indigenous traditions for his literary inspiration (in addition to *Leaves*, see, e.g., *The Adventures of Vela* [2009]). Recently, there has been an upsurge of interest in Indigenous literary voices. This upsurge is creating the conditions for a proper appreciation of Indigenous writers like Wendt. Indigenous criticism attests both to the historical damage to Indigenous cultures and to the survival of these cultures against great odds. As with Ngũgĩ, Wendt's literary work encompasses traditions of orature inherited from before colonialism; as with Ngũgĩ, properly assessing Wendt's work requires aesthetic principles that challenge normative, monocultural notions of literary value.

To be clear, my argument against literary monoculture does not require the wholesale rejection of global literary culture. That would seem to me as problematic a position as inattention to the literary/aesthetic traditions excluded by global literary culture. Rather than rejection, I aim at what one might call a deliberate vernacularization of global literary culture—that is, the recognition that this culture is just one among many that happens to have managed (problematically) to appropriate for itself a global literary space and then to claim paramount status in terms of value.

Literary values are not uniform. They don't remain the same over time or over geographical space. The temporal changeability of literary value is by now routinely accepted; few of us would assert that our idea of literary value is or should be that of Victorian England. The idea that a similar variation is observable contemporaneously across space is accepted less—or if accepted, the observation is not acted upon in any meaningful sense. We might speculate why this is the case—why the former is accepted and the latter mostly not. We might hypothesize that accepting our literary value is not the same as that of Victorian England does not require us to change how we go about recognizing literary greatness now. On the contrary, an acceptance of historical difference might even serve to confirm us in our modern conceptions of literary greatness.

However, to recognize the same kind of difference in valuing great works of literature among contemporary cultures spread across the globe—for example, to recognize that the contemporary Tamil world contains within it ideas about literary value completely alien to European and North American literary cultures—poses a direct challenge to whatever notions of greatness we might hold in the context of a global literary field. Where ideas of greatness do not align with the articulation of literary value in Tamil (or Japanese, or Hawaiian), which idea should prevail in the global literary field? And why? How, without provoking the charge of cultural imperialism, can we insist that any one literary value should be the standard? The contemporary diversity of literary value across geographical space poses these questions with an urgency not present in merely recognizing the historical changeability of literary value (from the past to the contemporary).

One way to respond seriously to these difficult questions is to foster the production of what I will call deep studies of the diversity of literary cultures. More particularly, one might conduct such studies as deep ethnographies of literary cultures. By this I mean the sustained and extensive study of the cultures of the literary, of interpretive communities of the literary, or, in yet another formulation, of the social formations through which ideas of the literary are produced, sustained, challenged, and transformed. Such ethnographies would surely help us understand literary cultures across the world much better than we do now.

Deep ethnographies can serve to foster knowledge of literary institutions and practices across the globe, especially in non-metropolitan spaces, whose literary cultures are so little known in metropolitan institutions. What might a deep ethnography of literary institutions and practices look like? And what might it teach us? These questions gain added urgency when we recognize that the assignation of literary value is historically and socially determined.

Like the best ethnography, these studies, if properly composed, would make no prejudgments about what is true literary value, thus allowing diverse ideas about literary value to be compared with one another dispassionately. Ethnographies of literary cultures, by expanding our knowledge of the great variety of institutions and practices of the literary and by exposing the social and historical processes working in the background, can save us from the trap of regarding the production of literary value as natural.

Biologists speak commonly of endangered species, and linguists of endangered languages. Biologists engage in practices to record and save endangered species, and linguists do the same for endangered languages. But what about endangered literary cultures? What do literary stakeholders owe endangered literary cultures? How do we record and save endangered literary cultures? Such questions are complex, and at a certain point the parallels with endangered species and languages fail.

Values, including literary values, are ideological: that is, they encode wide-ranging attitudes to the world. Accordingly, and unlike preserving the tiger, for example, saving literary cultures cannot be an innocent process. It is not an activity to engage in naively. Who would want to "save" a literary culture that is sexist, racist, or casteist? However, complexity—difficulty of the task before us—should not exempt us from acknowledging the basic points: that globally literary cultures are immensely diverse, and that many endangered literary cultures within this diversity have things to teach us. The global engagement with literature within this immense diversity through translation, anthologization, and similar literary practices is challenging but also exciting.

The 2025 Mānoa Journal *Contest Winner in Poetry*

JUDGED BY MAI DER VANG

WINNER, ERICA HOM

"Potent and unafraid in its offering of oral history, familial loss, and personal truth, this poem vividly bites back with a 'sharpness folded inward' that pays homage to matriarchal wisdom. The speaker's direct address compels the poem forward as each line moves with ease and intensity. What a powerful anthem and poem to live by!"

- Mai Der Vang

ERICA HOM

The Chinese word for endurance is the word for 'knife' atop the word 'heart'

Little girl, don't be afraid.   Catch the sky as it falls.
    Fold each fragment into a blanket.
When I had a fever,
    our stove became an altar.   Ninang stirred bitter herbs in
    a cauldron
    and prayed   Come sit.
Medicine; another sharpness we swallow
        Like how rain soaked earth swallows
    your brother's small coffin
    Your mother's sock drawer swallows a polaroid of a
    harelipped baby.
            For weeks, my mother swallows
        nothing.
In the garden, moth eaten spinach leaves
    Shake against the wind like bullet pierced flags.
Ninang slices open the red belly of a watermelon,
savors the sweetness   & spits away each dark seed.
Mother taught me to keep a knife under my pillow. Taught me
    how to measure rice
    with my sharpest knuckle.   Showed me which
    mushrooms
when consumed, could kill a man just in case.
Little girl, don't believe when they say
poison is a woman's weapon.

            I know it's whatever edge we hide within
        softness
        our sharpness folded inward.
This time, my mother hands me the blade.

The 2025 Mānoa Journal *Contest Runner-Up in Poetry*

JUDGED BY MAI DER VANG

RUNNER-UP, VINITA AGRAWAL

"Wrought with gorgeous language and emotional heft, this poem beautifully traverses the logistics of loss and duties involved with managing grief. Framing the poem are details of birds and animals that not only enrich the poem's meaning but also draw upon the mysteries and guardians of the natural world to aid in the process of crossing over."

- Mai Der Vang

VINITA AGRAWAL

Threshold Song

Guardians of the in-between,
the crows stitch the morning
with their slick, blue-black cries—
pin-striped shadows on winter-stripped trees.
They are everywhere, these watchers,
so plentiful we forget to listen.

There is so much waiting.
The hospice nurse's pen
hovers over the release papers
her voice steady as she teaches me
how to dissolve the last remnants of mercy
in a sink of cold water.
I whisper thanks to each vanishing pill—
tiny priests that eased her passage.

There is a loneliness in knowing too much,
in holding the paperwork,
in watching strangers wheel her away
while my wet hair drips onto my collar,
January air biting my neck.
The house is quiet now,
not because she sleeps,
but because absence has settled in.

Twenty years of sitting in silence
did not make death less sad.
Only softer.
Only this: a hand on my own shoulder,
my own voice saying it's alright,
there's nothing left to judge.

Outside, the crows riot—
a fox is near.
Their warnings overlap like echoes,
like the voices of those who've gone before,
urging stay, hide, wait.
I squint toward the den by the fence,
see nothing but frozen brush,
but I know—
something moves in the unseen.

The 2025 Mānoa Journal *Contest Winner in Fiction*

JUDGED BY MEGAN KAMALEI KAKIMOTO

WINNER, CHELSEA TOKUNO-LYNK

"The confident direct address in Tokuno-Lynk's 'The Good Girl's Guide to Boy Crazy' seized me from its first line, reading as much as a bidding as it does an invitation into a captivating narrative. The gorgeous specificity of images and unexpected details work in tandem with this brilliant voice to paint an indelible portrait of girlhood."

- Megan Kamalei Kakimoto

CHELSEA TOKUNO-LYNK

The Good Girl's Guide to Boy Crazy

You are a Good Girl. Your mother and grandmother never miss an opportunity to remind you that you are a Good Girl. Expect some version of this reminder after every family gathering, especially the ones with your older cousins in attendance, babies perched on their teenaged hips.

"You see how big Shani got?" your mom says on the drive back from Shani's baby shower. "That's why you gotta stay focused on school, Dana-girl. People call you goody-goody, so what? Better than you getting all boy crazy like Shani, then you get pregnant, then you get fat."

Fully embrace your Goodness. Be the only sophomore to take AP History and the only underclassman to make the varsity swim team. Spend your summer break hanging out with your best friend Charity at the Kaimukī Library, reading all the extra credit novels for next year's AP Lit class. Be the one to check on your dad whenever he passes out in front of the TV, a cluster of empty Heinekens on the coffee table. Smile at him when he unsticks his eyes open and calls you his Sweet Girl.

The first week of junior year, discover your capacity for boy crazy. ___ runs his hands through the short bob of your hair as you both wait in line for your student IDs. "You look cute, but kinda like a boy, you know," he tells you, his fingers tickling your neck. Feel thrilled and confused and intoxicated by the swell of heat rising in your body.

Confide in Charity about your new crush. She rolls her eyes and fake gags when you tell her. "Dana, he's an idiot," she says. But she shares a precalculus class with ___ and agrees to be your informant.

Remember you are a Good Girl. Convince yourself ___ is a Good Boy. You and ___ have known each other since you were eleven, before he grew eight inches and learned how to style his hair. You met as classmates in the sixth grade. Your first memory of him is of a little boy crouched down on the sidewalk, maneuvering the broad side of a plumeria leaf to escort a snail onto the grass so it would not be crushed by the afternoon stampede of middle schoolers. Cherish this memory. Wield it like a shield when Charity tells you he won't stop calling Ms. Lau, their math teacher, a chubby cow.

Pay attention to which girls ___ talks to in the lunch line. Don't despair when you notice he is always talking to Kahea Blanton or Bianca Kim or

Hannah Dang, all the girls in your class who are slim and trim and have nailed the sporty-but-girly look without even seeming to try. The kind of girls who aren't boy crazy but make the boys crazy. The kind of girls who get invited to cruise around Ala Moana on Friday afternoons with the seniors in the backseats of their cars. The kind of girls who aren't afraid to wear bikinis to the beach.

Grow out your hair even though it will be a pain in the ass to put on your swim cap at practice. Ask Charity to put in highlights so you show up to school with shocks of blonde that look terrific for two weeks until your chlorinated swim practices fade them to a dull, sickly green.

Stop eating white rice after seven o'clock. Your grandma tells you that late-night bowls of rice are why Auntie Jojo sprouted love handles in high school and could never get rid of them. Start paying attention to how far the meat of your thighs spreads on the metal benches during your swim coach's pep talks.

Try wearing shorts to school to show off the legs that Charity tells you are your best feature. ___ notices you for the first time in weeks, in the hallway after third period. "Hey, D," he says with a nod as you pass by. He smiles down at you, and you love the half-moons of his eyes as he grins. That night, he finds you on AIM for the first time in years. *Wassup?* Keep cool. Take five minutes to come up with your response. *Nothing much. U?* Wait an hour in the silence of your parents' living room. You hear your dad crack open a beer in the kitchen. Outside, an evening shower breaks open, and you smell the bloom of rain on asphalt through the open windows. ___ doesn't reply.

Start wearing shorts every day, always within dress code, even though your mom gives you an earful on your way out the door each morning, and your grandma says, "You better be keeping those legs shut, Dana-girl," when she picks you up after school.

Don't cry when your mom makes you cut three inches off because the highlights have shredded the ends of your hair. You hate how your hair looks now, flipping out at the tops of your broad swimmer's shoulders.

Don't despair when Charity tells you ___ is dating a volleyball player from McKinley High School. You will never be a volleyball star. You are not coordinated enough for ball sports, which is why you're on the swim team. You wonder if the volleyball player has long, lustrous hair that has been highlighted properly at a hair salon instead of in her best friend's bathroom sink. You wonder if she has the same thick, shapely legs as you, or if she has kissed ___ yet with her tongue.

Over winter break, swipe your mom's Dido CD and listen to the songs on repeat to cope with not seeing ___ for two whole weeks. Your crush has not dulled despite the knowledge that he currently belongs to the volleyball player. Your headphones muffle the sound of your parents arguing about your dad's habit of drinking one, two, three bottles of beer with dinner every night. Stare at your bedroom ceiling and gorge yourself on the delicious ache of unrequited affection.

When you finally see ___ on AIM on Christmas of all nights, do not hesitate to message him. *Hey, Merry Christmas. How's ur break?* Fall asleep to "White Flag" and a crying jag when he doesn't message you back.

Resolve to be a Different Person when you go back to school in the new year. Remember you are a Good Girl. Swear off the boy crazy. Start wearing jeans and sweats to school again; the weather chilling anyway. Wear your hair tied back in a stub of a ponytail. You need to get your head right for the spring ACT test and the last swim meet of the season. When you see ___ in the hallway, resist the urge to make eye contact. Feel as if you have passed a small test.

Buckle down with an ACT prep course you attend every Thursday after school. Wring your lungs out swimming sprints during practice.

Pretend you feel nothing when Charity calls you at your grandma's house and tells you ___ has split with the volleyball player. "He didn't seem too bummed. I think he broke it off. But you're over him, anyway, right?" Twist the phone cord into knots around your finger. Tell her, "Yeah, no, I'm over it." "Good. He's still an idiot. Oh, and he's gonna start taking that ACT prep class. Apparently he got like a 12 the last time. Y'know, because he's an idiot."

Be unbothered when ___ shows up at the next ACT prep course. When he chooses to sit beside you, let yourself look him in the face as you say hi. Register the smell of his body spray. Suddenly the room is too warm for your sweatpants. You wish you had worn shorts. Let him borrow your pencil. Let him offer you a perfectly shaped cookie out of a Ziploc bag. He is the type to pack afternoon snacks, and this melts something inside you. "I made em," he says. "They're really good," you say, and then realize too late he is joking.

Be surprised by the ease you find in his company on Thursday afternoons. Find out you both watch the new J-drama that's been airing on the local Japanese channel. Impress him with the fact that you taught yourself hiragana over the winter break. Realize that maybe you are friends. Except for the kaleidoscope of butterflies that beat against your rib cage when he sketches the shape of your mouth on his workbook and tells you, "You know your mouth curves. Right here."

When ___ doesn't show up for the last ACT prep class, feel hurt, then devastated when Charity tells you he was suspended for drinking on campus.

Find him on AIM. Do not be surprised when he responds right away. You are friends now, after all. Tell him about your father's multiple DUIs even though your mom made you swear not to tell anyone, not even your grandma. *It's dumb. I got 2 take alcohol education classes.* You agree with Charity; he is an idiot, but your weeks of shared Thursday afternoons make you feel a ballooned allegiance to him. *That sucks*, you reply, even though you hope and pray he doesn't drink again until he is thirty.

Brace for the end of your swim season that hits like a storm. You have no time for AIM sessions. The one night you log on, he isn't even online. You don't see or talk to him for three whole weeks.

Swallow your sadness when ___ finally returns from his suspension sentence, but you no longer see him on a reliable, regular basis. ACT prep courses are over; the spring ACT has already come and gone. When you do pass in the hallway, you trade stiff nods. You want to ask him how he's doing, but you can't figure out how. You're not sure if you're even friends anymore.

Don't get your hopes up when bids come out for junior prom. Ask Charity to ask ___ if he's planning on going, if he has a date. Don't be disappointed when she tells you he has already asked Hannah Dang.

When Dylan Lee asks you to prom, say yes. Dylan is a friend, decent and sweet, and most importantly has his own car, a secondhand Camry that wheezes a little when it brakes. Say yes because you want to go. Say yes because Charity will be there too, and some of your swim teammates, and it will be a Good Time. Say yes because you want to torture yourself watching ___ dance all night with slim and trim Hannah Dang, with her long hair like a waterfall and her backless gold dress.

On prom night, let your parents take photos of you and Dylan Lee on your front lawn. The sun is setting, and your mom wants to capture you, all dressed up, framed against the slopes of Pālolo Valley behind your house. Your dress is a tight, strappy thing that disguises your broad shoulders and shows off too much leg for your grandma's tastes, but she joins your mom in taking at least a hundred photos of you and Dylan Lee. Try to ignore the neighbors smiling at you as they water their yard. Dylan looks nice enough, though he is the same height as you in your heels. Present him with a single-strand maile lei and accept his bouquet of roses, red to match your dress. When Dylan tells you that you look beautiful, clamp down on your cringe and say thank you.

Prom is in the third-floor ballroom of a Waikīkī hotel. It is the fanciest party you've ever attended. Force yourself to have a Good Time, even after you find out your table is right next to ___ and Hannah Dang, who looks unfairly stunning with her perfect tan and cleavage. The attraction you feel to ___ dressed up in a tux is outrageous. You don't trust yourself to look at him more than once. Though you can't help but notice Hannah Dang constantly touching his leg during dinner, and you try not to laugh when Charity pretends to hurl into her water glass.

Don't feel bad about telling Dylan you don't feel like dancing. Hang out with your teammates along the ballroom balcony that overlooks the twinkling stretch of Waikīkī and try not to feel like a wallflower. Don't watch the dance floor, where you know Hannah Dang is putting all her moves on ___.

Don't panic when Charity finds you halfway through the night with the guiltiest look on her face. Try not to scream when she tells you she accidentally told ___ you had a big crush on him. Demand to know how this was an accident. Relax a little when she reveals Hannah ditched him on the dance floor when her ex, Keoni Higa, asked her to leave with him early. "I told him because, I dunno, I thought it would make him feel better about being dumped."

Resist the urge to run when you see ___ walking toward you on the balcony, the top of his tux unbuttoned, the breeze blowing in from the beachfront tousling his hair. He looks like a dream. You feel tongue-tied and ridiculous.

Let him invite you on a walk to a quieter corner along the balcony. Let him stand closer to you than he has since your last ACT prep class together. Let him ask you, "Is Charity for real? You used to like me?" Don't lie. Nod your head. Tug at a strand of hair that has fallen out of your updo. Let him touch your bottom lip, the one he sketched in his workbook. Let him tug you forward and pull you in for a kiss that is too much spit, too much muscular tongue, too much teeth. Don't tell him he doesn't taste good.

Try to look anything but confused when he pulls back and asks you what you got on the ACT. Tell him the truth because what else would you say? You were three points shy of a perfect score. "You're so smart, Dana." Try not to look upset when he pulls out a tiny bottle of alcohol, like the ones you've seen your dad tuck into his front pocket at the grocery store checkout. Tell him no when he offers you some. Realize that the sour flavor you tasted in his mouth was liquor. Try your best to look neutral when he rambles, "You taking the ACT again? Take it again, D; we can take it at the same time, yeah? You can help me, yeah?" Try not to push him away when he leans in for your mouth again.

Let Dylan Lee drop you off at home at midnight. Thank him for the ride. Have the decency to feel a little bad for ditching him most of prom. Thank him for the Good Time. Tell your mom, who has waited up for you bleary-eyed in the living room, your father already asleep in their bed for once, that you had a Good Time.

In your own bed, let yourself cry even though you don't know why you feel so embarrassed. You can still feel the force of ___'s fingers between your legs. You can still feel the heat of his breath on your face.

Tell Charity you are officially over ___. When she asks why, tell her he asked you to help him cheat on the ACT. "What an idiot," she says. Don't tell her about the tiny bottle of alcohol or the way he pushed his hand between your legs. Pretend that never happened.

Start swimming laps for hours after school, even though the season is over, because full immersion in water is the only time you feel clean. When you see ___ around campus and the butterflies still tickle your stomach, remind yourself you are a Good Girl.

Vinita Agrawal has authored six books of poetry. Books edited by her include two anthologies on climate change, *The Centennial Volume on Nissim Ezekiel - Poet & Father* and a Kashmiri anthology. Her poem won an award at Brew Poetry in 2025. She also received the third prize from the Science Fiction and Fantasy Poetry Association (SFPA) in 2025. She is the recipient of the Jayanta Mahapatra National Award for Literature 2024, the Proverse Prize Hongkong 2021, the Rabindranath Tagore Literary Prize 2018, and the Gayatri GaMarsh Memorial Award for Literary Excellence, USA, 2015. Her book *Eartha* was long listed for the Sarojini Naidu Award for Poetry 2025. She won a special mention in the Hawkers Prize 2019. She coedits the Yearbook series of Indian Poetry in English. She was former Poetry Editor with *Usawa Literary Review*. She is on the Advisory Board of the Tagore Literary Prize. She is the author of a children's fiction book. Her work has been published in *Global South, Mascara Review, Indian Literature, Asian Cha, The Bombay Literary Magazine*, and the *Knopf Newsletter, Canary, Tabula Rasa, Chrysalis Blue*, and *Madras Courier*, among others. She is a birder and a photographer. www.vinitawords.com.

Siddhesh Gautam is an India-based multidiscipline, mixed-media artist, designer, writer, poet, dreamer, storyteller, and an Ambedkarite. His work is currently focused on the visual documentation of the anti-caste movement, global warming and gender equality. His work has been published in organizations such as *BBC, The Guardian, Hyperallergic, The Funambulist Magazine*, etc. He has also worked with and given lectures and talks at various universities and colleges including Stanford University, University of Washington, Oxford University, SOAS University of London, University of Vienna and International Institute of Social Studies, Hague.

Erica Hom is a Filipina-diaspora poet, artist, and educator. Her writing has been featured in various online magazines, art installations, and print publications, including *West Trade Review, Room Magazine, The Arkansas International, Honey Literary, Sidewalk Poetry, Voices from the Attic*, and the *Midway Journal*. Her work was awarded the CD Wright's Emerging Poets Prize and was twice nominated for *Best of the Net*.

Joel Lee is the author of *Deceptive Majority: Dalits, Hinduism and Underground Religion* (Cambridge University Press, 2021) and coeditor, with K. Satyanarayana, of *Concealing Caste: Passing and Personhood in Dalit Literature* (Oxford University Press, 2023). He teaches anthropology at Williams College in Massachusetts.

Prof. **Maya Pandit** retired from the EFL University, Hyderabad, after thirty-nine years of teaching and research in Translation Studies, English Language Education, and Feminist Criticism. She has translated many works (essays, plays, novels, poems, and autobiographies), including English translations of Marathi Dalit women's autobiographies, viz., Baby Kamble's *The Prisons We Broke*, Urmila Pawar's *The Weave of My Life*, Jayant Pawar's Marathi play *The Nowhere People*, polemical texts like Mahatma Phule's *Slavery* and Saniya's *Novelette.* She also translated Krishnat Khot's award-winning novel *Ringaan* as *Ringaan: The Full Circle.* Her Marathi translations of English plays include Dario Fo's *An Accidental Death of an Anarchist*, Dario Fo and Franca Rame's *Awakening*, Ramu Ramnathan's *Mahadevbhai*, and Biswajit Das's *Mrugaya.* Her original works include works on Gopal Ganesh Agarkar and Govind Purushottam Deshpande in English and a Marathi poetry collection, *Talkhali.* Recipient of several fellowships, she directed a documentary film on Marathi Dalit Women Writers for Sahitya Akademi, *Voices from the Margins.* An ardent activist in the Marathi alternative theatre and women's movement, she has participated in several national and international seminars and published several research papers.

Anushiya Ramaswamy grew up in Colombo, Sri Lanka, and is currently a professor of English at Southern Illinois University Edwardsville. She teaches Theory of Composition, Rhetoric, and African American Literature. Anushiya's work has appeared in *World Literature Today* and *Callaloo*, and she has translated the Sri Lankan Tamil writer Shobasakthi's novels, *Gorilla* and *Traitor*, and short stories published as *The MGR Murder Trial.* She has also translated the Tamil Dalit poet N. D. Rajkumar's poetry, *Give Us This Day a Feast of Flesh.* Her translations of the Sri Lankan-born Canadian-Tamil poet Cheran's poems have appeared in various venues. Anushiya was also one of the three translators of the international poetry collection, *In Our Translated World: Contemporary Global Tamil Poetry*, published in Toronto, Canada. Her translations of Shobasakthi's novels *Box: A Novel* and *Ichaa* are both forthcoming from Navayana Publishers, New Delhi. Anushiya is currently translating Shobasakthi's latest novel, *Salaam Alaik.*

K. Satyanarayana is Professor in the Department of Cultural Studies at the English and Foreign Languages University, Hyderabad. He has designed and taught a set of courses under the rubric "Dalit Studies" and has published books and essays in the broad field of Dalit intellectual and literary history.

He has coedited two volumes of new Dalit writing: *No Alphabet in Sight* (Penguin, 2011) and *Steel Nibs Are Sprouting* (Harper Collins, 2013) and the critical anthologies *Dalit Studies* (Duke UP, 2016), *Dalit Text* (2020), and, most recently, *Concealing Caste* (Oxford UP, 2023). At present, he is most interested in thinking about questions of dignity and equality in Indian literary cultures, intellectual traditions, and cultural practices. He teaches courses on cultural theory, Indian cultural history, and Dalit studies.

S. Shankar is a novelist, literary and cultural critic, and translator. He is Professor at the Department of English, University of Hawai'i at Mānoa; Editor of *Mānoa* journal; and a former member of the Board of External Experts appointed to advise the Swedish Academy in the awarding of the Nobel Prize for Literature (2022–2025). Shankar's most recent book is his third novel, *Ghost in the Tamarind* (2017). His volume of criticism, *The Cost of Living: The Stories We Tell about the Poor*, is forthcoming (Duke University Press, 2027). Shankar is the translator of Komal Swaminathan's play *Thaneer, Thaneer* (Water!) and other works from Tamil.

Amme Shirisha grew up in Telangana, India. Shirisha did her undergraduate degree in Combined Humanities at Azim Premji University, Bangalore. She finished her Master's from IIT Gandhinagar in M.A. Society and Culture. Her translation of Ravi Shastry's book, "Six Liquor Stories," is yet to be published.

Chelsea Tokuno-Lynk is a writer and nonprofit fundraiser, and the great-grandchild of Japanese farmers and laborers in Hawai'i and the Bay Area. She grew up in Kāne'ohe, Hawai'i, and now lives in Milwaukee, Wisconsin, with her spouse and two children. With her work supported by the Virginia Center of the Creative Arts, VONA/Voices, and Kundiman, her stories have appeared in *Joyland, The Iowa Review*, and elsewhere.

Note: Information on the translated authors in *Touchable/Untouchable* can be found elsewhere in this issue.